SYLVIA'S SPIRIT

Oregon Sky Book Five

KAY P. DAWSON

Sylvia's Spirit: Oregon Sky Book Five
Paperback version

CKN Christian Publishing
An Imprint of Wolfpack Publishing
5130 S. Fort Apache Rd. 215-380
Las Vegas, NV 89148

cknchristianpublishing.com

Print ISBN 978-1-63977-229-2

SYLVIA'S SPIRIT

CHAPTER 1

"No! Duncan, wake up!" Sylvia fell to her knees beside the man she'd married only a few short hours ago, even though she already knew he wasn't waking up. She tried to shake him, not letting her eyes move to the puddle of blood around the back of his head. "You can't just leave me here like this. I don't know anyone and I have nowhere to go. Please, wake up!"

She fought against the hysteria that was building as her eyes darted all around her to see what she could use to help him. There had to be something she could do.

Her gaze was pulled to the large rock lying on the other side of Duncan. *Was that blood on it?*

Reaching out, she lifted it and brought her hand to her mouth to cover the sob that escaped.

Her hand shook as she held it, knowing somehow her husband must have tripped and fallen, hitting his head on this rock.

Even in her rattled mind, she couldn't help wondering how he could have possibly gone down hard enough to be killed from the fall. Surely if he'd called out for help she would have heard him.

Guilt ate at her as she sat back on the ground, still firmly gripping the rock. *She wouldn't have heard him.* He could have been lying here for the past two hours calling for help. But she'd fallen asleep and had only woken up a few minutes ago. As soon as she'd noticed Duncan wasn't in the house, she'd come out looking for him.

The trip west had played her out and when she'd finally had a moment to sit on a bed and relax, she'd succumbed to her tired body. She was only going to close her eyes for a quick rest but once she'd fallen asleep, she was gone and she was certain nothing would have woken her up.

"What have you done?"

A man's voice shouted from behind her and the sudden wailing of a woman's voice joined in. Sylvia leaped to her feet, spinning around to face whoever had joined her. She assumed it would be the brother and stepmother Duncan had told her lived in a small cabin on the property. Her heart was racing as she tried to sort through everything that was happening.

"He...he must have fallen and hit his head. I can't get him to wake up." Her voice shook as she spoke, so she swallowed hard to try to get herself under control. The woman had flung herself on the ground beside Duncan while the man pushed her to the side to reach his brother. He crouched down and held his hand on Duncan's chest, then dropped his head and shook it.

The woman started crying harder, grabbing Duncan's hand in hers. "No, not my boy. Duncan, no!"

Sylvia's eyes filled with tears again as the pain in the woman's voice tore at her heart.

"I'm so sorry, Mrs. Coulter. I just came out to find him and he was on the ground..."

"*Liar!*" The woman had lifted her head and yelled the word so quickly Sylvia didn't even have time to react.

The brother stood up and faced her, looking down at the rock she still held in her hand. "Do you expect us to believe you didn't do this? Even while you stand there holding the very thing that just killed my brother?" he hissed the words out angrily and shook his head. "No. You killed him because you only came out here to marry him for the money. I warned him about doing this but he wouldn't listen. Now look where that's got him." He thrust his hand toward Duncan lying on the ground.

He was slowly walking toward her, sneering in anger.

"No! I didn't kill him, I swear! I fell asleep when he came outside to do the chores and when I woke up he still wasn't in the house, so I came looking for him. I found him like this." The world around her was starting to spin as she looked down at Duncan, then to the woman who was now glaring at her with hatred, and back to his brother in front of her. They were devastated and angry at what they'd just found. Surely, they'd listen to her once they'd had time for the shock to wear off.

But even as she thought it, she somehow knew they were beyond listening to reason. When Duncan's brother reached out to grab her arm, instinctively she pulled away, stepping back.

"Please, just listen to me. I would never have hurt Duncan. I'd barely even had a chance to know him."

"I don't believe you. You can tell it to the judge and see what he thinks, although after witnessing what both my mother and I walked into, I have no doubt the law will agree with us. You came out here to marry my brother, then killed him as soon as you had what you wanted." He started moving toward her again. "But you won't get away with it. I won't rest until I see you hang."

Her breath caught in her throat as she realized just how serious this man was. He believed she'd killed his brother and he wanted her to pay. She had no way to prove otherwise.

He grabbed at the rock in her hand. "And I'm sure the judge will want to see exactly what you used to do it."

Her eyes moved to the blood-stained rock he now held in front of him. Her chin quivered as she tried not to think about the fact that it was her husband's blood she was looking at. Only a few short hours ago she'd met the man she'd been corresponding with and had been married in the small church in town as soon as she'd stepped off the stagecoach.

She'd had a chance to see promise for her future and the belief that perhaps someone could grow to love and care for her in time. She was finally going to have a home and a family of her own.

And now, those chances had been ripped from her grasp.

Instead, she was going to have to defend herself against a crime she never committed, in a town where no one knew her or cared who she was, and with no way of proving her innocence.

Life hadn't always been good for her but this was the first time she'd ever felt truly alone and without hope. Without thinking, she turned to run. She had to get away to give herself a chance. Maybe she could just get far enough away and start a new life where no one could find her.

Her heart pounding in her ears, she tried to run but her legs were like lead. She realized with a sad twist in her heart that she was still wearing the simple white blouse she'd put on to be married in.

It seemed like nothing wanted to work properly in her body and before she knew what was happening, a heavy weight slammed into her, knocking her to the ground. "You're not getting away. And as far as anyone knows, you and my brother weren't even married. So you can forget about getting any of his money or possessions."

As she'd fallen, her cheek had struck a hard branch poking from the ground and she could feel a warm trickle slowly making its way over her skin. She twisted to try to get the man's heavy weight off her body. "I don't want anything from him. You can have all of it. I would never have killed someone just for their money." She tried moving again, his heavy weight starting to hurt her legs.

"We'll let the judge, and the good citizens of Bethany, decide whether that's true or not. For now, you'll be spending your first night in town with the new sheriff. I'm not letting you get away with what you've done."

He moved off her to stand up and she was finally able to breathe again. But he wasn't letting go of her arms and he yanked her up to stand beside him. She winced as pain shot through her shoulder. Her hair had fallen down around her face and she struggled to see through the tears that were filling her eyes.

No one was going to believe her. She was a strange woman who'd just arrived in town and whose husband had just mysteriously died.

Would there be anyone she could trust who would be willing to give her a fighting chance?

CHAPTER 2

"Grace, you should have just gone home with Phoebe and Colton. Now I have to make sure you get home safely before the nightly antics at the saloon get going." Luke turned around to latch the door, ignoring the grin on his little sister's face.

"You know perfectly well you like it when you have to take me home because then you get a good home-cooked meal."

He smiled to himself as he turned to take her arm and escort her over to where their horses were tethered. Of course, his sister had chosen to ride in on the horse today, instead of the wagon like a sensible person would do. Since she'd arrived in Oregon a few years ago, Grace had been living on the Wallace farmstead with his other sister Phoebe and her husband Colton. Grace was known to spend most of her days on the back of her horse.

He tried to ignore the familiar twinge of guilt he felt whenever he thought about how Phoebe had been forced to take care of Grace after their parents died. He hadn't been there when their father was killed and then he hadn't stepped up to take responsibility of them when he should have.

By then, Phoebe had fallen in love with Colton and it had just been easier to let them look after Grace.

But the guilt was still there and he figured it always would be.

Putting his arm around Grace's shoulders, Luke led her along the wooden sidewalk to the horses. "Well, I guess you're right about that. I would never turn down a home-cooked meal. It sure beats the beans and runny eggs I'd be getting over at Frank's."

Frank Tanner had opened the new saloon up the street a few months ago and since Luke had taken on the sheriff's job in town, he'd been eating his meals between there and Dorothy Larsen's boardinghouse. Luke lived in a small room above the building that had been built to house the sheriff's office when the growing town of Bethany had decided they were big enough to need someone keeping order. But it didn't have much in it and there wasn't the room to try cooking any of his own meals.

It wasn't much but it was the first place he'd really been able to call home in a long time.

He stopped by his horse and let his eyes move up and down the street, taking everything in. The sun was still high enough in the sky to give off some heat, letting them all know that winter was over and it was now time to enjoy the warmth of spring.

"Thanks for letting me stay and help out today. I like getting to spend time with my brother, even if he is annoying and bossy."

He tipped his head down slightly, raising his eyebrow at the smiling face staring up at him. His arm still rested around her shoulders, her blonde hair tickling his skin.

"I wouldn't have to be bossy if you could just do things the way I ask you to the first time."

Grace rolled her eyes. "I really don't see what difference it makes if I fold the cover down neatly on the cot in the cell. Even drunken criminals deserve to have a nice place to lay their heads at night."

Luke shook his head, laughter escaping from

his lips. "Well, it still seems like a waste of time to me."

It had become a habit for Grace to stay in and help out around his office whenever Phoebe or Colton came into town for supplies. He'd only been the sheriff for a couple of months now and he welcomed her help to keep things neat and tidy around his small office while he took over the law enforcement duties in town.

Bethany had never had the need for a lawman until now. Once the saloon opened and with more settlers coming west to stake their claims to land, the once small town had continued to grow. There was even a doctor in town now which saved the residents from having to go to Oregon City.

When the residents had brought up the need for a sheriff at one of their local church meetings, Luke's name had been thrown out as one of the best candidates for the job. He'd spent most of the past few years making his way around the country, doing jobs here and there as needed. But he'd recently decided to stay in Bethany where both his sisters now lived. He needed something more stable.

He wasn't married and didn't have anything that would keep him from doing an important job like being sheriff. No one came right out and said it but he suspected the fact he didn't have any children to leave behind if something should happen to him was also a factor they'd considered.

Either way, he was happy for the new job. It was one he planned to do his best at, and he wanted to make sure the residents were never sorry for hiring him.

Just as he was about to help his sister onto her horse, a voice shouted from the end of the street leading from town. Stepping back to get a better look, a wagon kicked up dust as it flew toward them.

"Sheriff Hamilton! We've got someone here you need to lock up."

He cringed slightly as he realized it was Duncan Coulter's brother, Randolph. The man had shown up in town with their mother a couple of months after Duncan arrived a year ago. While Duncan had become a well-liked member of the community, the brother had kept to himself and not bothered to hide his disdain for this small town.

There weren't many people in town who liked him, including Luke. He wasn't sure if it was the way he put on a show of kindness that never quite reached his eyes or the way the man had started eyeing up his little sister any time she was around town.

As the wagon came to a stop in front of the sheriff's office, the dust hung in the air around them like a cloak. His mother Winnie was seated stoically next to him, her hands folded neatly in front of her on her lap. She didn't appear to have even one hair out of place or wrinkle caused from the breakneck speed they'd just been doing.

Luke walked back over to stand in front of the office while Randolph jumped down from the wagon and ran over to him. "You need to arrest this woman. She just killed my brother and I want to make sure she pays."

Luke looked to Winnie sitting on the seat. "Your mother?" He'd always suspected the man might be a slight bit touched in the head but the way he was carrying on now was taking away any remaining doubts.

Randolph grabbed his arm and pulled him around to the back. "No, this hussy who came into town today to marry my brother and kill him within a few hours of saying her vows."

Luke was desperately trying to follow what the man was saying but nothing was making sense. When he got to the back of the wagon, he gasped at the sight of a woman tied up in the back wearing a white blouse and plain skirt that was now covered in dirt and blood.

She was lying on the hard, wooden floorboards with dried blood spread across her cheek. Her eyes were closed but, as he stood staring in shock, she slowly opened them and met his.

He couldn't tell for sure what color they were from where he stood. All he could see was the pain and hopelessness in the watery stare that held him in its grip.

She hadn't even moved since the wagon had stopped as though she knew there was no point in fighting. Her dress was torn around her arms and he had to fight the fury that rose as his eyes moved to her wrists that had been rubbed raw from the tight rope binding them together.

When Randolph jumped into the back of the wagon and reached down to yank her to standing, Luke couldn't take anymore.

"Get your hands off that woman now and step out of the wagon."

The man looked at him with his mouth gaping. "I won't. This woman killed Duncan."

"I don't care if she killed the King of England. Take your hands off her now."

Luke knew he wasn't thinking clearly—if the

woman *had* killed Duncan Coulter, then she did have to face the law. But no one deserved to be roughed up and handled like this. And by the looks of her, she hadn't been treated kindly while getting thrown into the wagon.

Randolph sneered as he pushed the woman toward Luke. She stumbled over the rope that held her legs together and started to fall. Luke reached out and pulled her into his arms before she fell onto the ground.

Looking down into her eyes, his breath caught in his chest. He'd never seen eyes such a deep brown. And as she looked back at him, he could see the tears that she'd been holding back.

"I never killed anyone."

Her voice was low but held a strength that surprised him. Even after what she'd obviously just been through, he noticed a spark behind the wetness of her tears that showed she wasn't going to just let them accuse her of something like this without a fight.

For some reason, he found himself hoping beyond hope that what she was saying was true. And he was determined to do whatever it took to help her prove it.

CHAPTER 3

Sylvia stood with her back to the bars, staring at the wall. The sheriff was trying to calm everyone down, but it seemed like the more he tried, the angrier Duncan's family was getting. One thing she'd learned over the years was that trying to argue or have someone listen when they were this angry never worked.

It looked like she was going to have plenty of time with the sheriff to try telling her side of the story anyway. So she would wait until Duncan's brother and his mother left before saying her piece.

"No, you listen to me Randolph. I know you're angry and upset about your brother. I'd be furious if I were in your shoes. But you can't just tie a woman up and toss her in your wagon like she's a sack of flour. She's half the size of you. She wasn't going to be able to put up much of a fight anyway."

She cringed slightly as Randolph laughed. "Shows how much you know. That girl in there kicked me so hard I almost saw stars. And look at these claw marks where she scratched me."

She allowed herself a moment to gloat, knowing she'd made the man bleed as he'd started tying her up. She'd figured, at that point, if he wasn't going to listen to reason then she was going to at least make him suffer like she was.

"Well, I'd have done the same if you were tying me up."

The sheriff's voice sounded angry and she was surprised that he was defending her actions. Most men stuck together, so she'd been sure he'd believe everything this man was telling him right away.

But for some reason, this sheriff seemed different. When he'd caught her as she fell from the wagon, she'd sensed a kindness she hoped was truly there. He'd carried her into the sheriff's office while Randolph had been yelling behind him to make sure she was locked up tight. He'd just ignored the other man and carefully set her down on the small cot inside the cell.

Before he'd stood back up, he'd offered her a smile. "I'm going to have to lock you in here until I get everything sorted out. It's just easier than having to listen to Randolph hollering that I'm not doing my job. But, I'll get you a cloth as soon as I can, so you can get yourself cleaned up a bit."

Then he'd stood up to face Duncan's family. The words they'd been calling her stung but she tried not to listen. She knew they were hurt and angry, so she couldn't really be upset with them. Maybe once they had some time to think about it, they'd be more willing to listen to her.

"Here, Luke told me to bring you a cloth and some water. I know he'll make sure someone picks up your clothes and brings them to you once he gets things settled down here."

Sylvia spun around at the sound of the female voice behind her. A young woman, who looked close to her own age, stood smiling at her as she held a basin and cloth in her outstretched hand on the other side of the bars.

"I'm Grace, Sheriff Hamilton's sister." Grace nodded toward her hands. "You should wash your cuts and bruises off, so you don't get any infection."

Realizing the other woman was only trying to help her, Sylvia let go of the breath she'd been holding. Her eyes quickly darted past Grace to where the sheriff was still trying to calm Duncan's family down enough to figure out what was going on.

Grace was right. She needed to clean herself up, so she could be presentable when she finally had the chance to give her side of the story. No one was going to believe she was innocent while she was covered in blood.

She went over and took the cloth and basin from Grace. "Thank you. I appreciate it."

Suddenly feeling the emotions of the day starting to well up inside her, she quickly swallowed against the lump that formed in her throat.

Grace pulled a chair up beside the bars and sat down. "I know things look pretty bad right now but I know my brother and he'll be fair. If you didn't do anything, he'll do everything he can to help you prove it."

Sylvia wrung the cloth out and brought it up to her face. She closed her eyes, letting the coolness of the water ease the sting of her wounds. The fight she'd tried to put up against Duncan's brother hadn't ended well in her favor. And then being flung onto the wooden floorboards for the trip to town had left her with cuts and slivers she was sure would never heal.

When she pulled the cloth down to dip back into the water, she gasped at the redness of it.

Lifting her eyes to Grace, she couldn't stop the tears that blurred her vision. "Is it bad?"

She almost didn't want to know. It was hard enough as a woman on your own in the world but a woman with a disfigured face would meet even more difficulty.

That's if she ever got her freedom again.

Grace shook her head. "Just a few scratches and bruises. Nothing a little time won't heal." She smiled and Sylvia could feel the genuine compassion in the other woman's eyes. At least she might have one friend out here.

"I don't care what you do, Sheriff, but you better be sending for the judge, so we can see her pay. I'm not letting her get away with this."

"I find it very difficult to believe a woman of this size could kill your brother. I met Duncan many times over the past year since he moved to Bethany and he wasn't a small man."

"Are you calling my son a liar?"

Duncan's stepmother was sitting in a chair with her hands on her lap.

The sheriff sighed and pushed his hand through his hair, almost knocking his large-brimmed hat from his head.

"I'm not calling anyone anything. I just need to listen to the facts and try to make sense of everything. And right now, none of this makes any sense to me." Suddenly, he turned, and his eyes met her, sending a shock right down to her core. She'd never seen eyes as intense as his.

"Why would this woman come out here to marry a man and then kill him before the ink had even dried on the license?"

His stare stayed on her as though he was trying to see what she was thinking. The brightness of his eyes almost made her believe he could.

"Because she wanted his money. And now she thinks she's got it." Randolph walked over and sneered at her through the bars. "But you'll never see a penny of my brother's money. I doubt any judge in the world would recognize your marriage after only a few short hours."

Luke walked over and stood beside the other man, finally taking his eyes off hers. "Well, if they were married in the church, then it doesn't matter what any judge thinks. As long as there's a license signed by your brother, the marriage will be legal."

Duncan's brother was still glaring at her. "How do we even know they were married? Seems funny that he wouldn't have invited his own family to witness the blessed event."

Sylvia clenched her fist around the cloth. "I assure you, we were married. If you don't believe me, you can ask Reverend Johnson. I'm sure he'd be glad to show you the papers."

Randolph threw his head back and laughed. "Reverend Johnson? That old codger wouldn't remember what he did five minutes ago. No judge in his right mind would take anything he says into account."

Luke put his hand on Randolph's shoulder. "Well, it's a good thing there'll be paperwork if the marriage took place. And if she's proven innocent, then as his wife, she'll be entitled to anything your brother had unless he had a will stating otherwise. But that's not the issue right now. We need to figure out exactly what happened on your farm today."

Those eyes found hers again and she knew this was her one chance to make him believe her.

Because if he didn't, she didn't know who else would be able to help her.

CHAPTER 4

"Grace will bring you something to change into when she comes back in the morning. I've asked her to come first thing. For now, you're welcome to put this on for the night." He reached through the bars of the cell and handed the woman a plaid, flannel shirt he had in the office. "It'll keep you warm too. I'm afraid it gets a bit chilly in here overnight."

She gave him a half-smile as she took the shirt from his hand. "Thank you. I'd like to get this blouse off."

He looked at the torn shoulder of the blouse he was sure had been beautiful before she'd been roughed up by Randolph. "I'll give you some privacy." Turning his back to her, he went and stood looking out the window to the street, so she could get changed.

His mind was racing with the events that had unfolded in the past couple of hours. After Randolph and his mother gave their statements, he'd had to convince them to leave and let him take care of things from here. Then he'd gone over to the O'Hara's mercantile and asked James, a good friend of the family, to escort Grace home before it got dark.

Now he had to figure out where to go from here. Since he'd become the sheriff in Bethany, there hadn't been any serious cases to deal with. The most he'd had to handle was the odd man who'd had a bit too much at the saloon and thought they would settle a dispute with their fists.

He knew he'd have to get a message to the traveling judge who would then decide if she should face trial or what her future would be. But the judge wasn't due back in this area for over a week, so he hoped it would give him some time to find out the truth of what happened.

"You can turn around now."

Her voice startled him but he turned back to face her, prepared to sit down and hear her side of things now. But when he saw her standing there wearing his large shirt hanging down over her skirt, it took him a moment to catch his breath. There was just something so intimate in knowing his shirt was touching her skin.

Giving his head a shake, he stopped where his thoughts were going. This woman was a potential murderer. It wasn't a good idea to look at her as anything more than that. He couldn't let himself be swayed by the fact she was a beautiful woman underneath all those scratches and bruises.

"I can't imagine how I must look right now. I appreciate the shirt, though, even if it's a bit big." She smiled nervously at him as she tried to roll the sleeves up that were hanging down over her hands.

"Well, I'd imagine you've had a bit of a rough day, so I don't think you should be worrying how you look." He saw the torn blouse lying on the cot where she'd thrown it. "If you want to give me your blouse, I guess I'll have to hold onto it for when the judge comes around."

She looked down at it and closed her eyes tightly for a few seconds. "I saved my money to buy that blouse so I'd have something nice to wear when I married Duncan."

Her voice was barely above a whisper. She finally reached down and picked it up, then walked over to hand it to him through the bars. When her eyes met his, he saw a flicker of anger. "Make sure the judge knows the blood on this shirt is my own. It was still in perfect shape until Randolph decided to rough me up as punishment for a crime I never committed."

He took the blouse and looked down at it, anger starting to boil in his chest at the possibility she was telling the truth. If she was, then she'd suffered at the hands of Randolph before she got here. However, she could also be lying to him and playing him for a fool. It could just as easily be Duncan's blood.

Setting the blouse on his desk, he pulled a chair up next to the cell. "Now that everyone else is gone, why don't you give me your side of what happened today?"

She lifted her chin higher and clasped her hands in front of her waist. "Are you going to believe me anyway? I've tried to tell the truth of what happened today but no one seemed intent on listening."

He could understand her anger and frustration. "I'm not Randolph. I'm sworn to uphold the law and that means taking everything into account and deciding what is true and what isn't. I promise if you tell me the truth, I'll be fair."

She swallowed and brought her arms up to hug her chest. "About a year ago I answered an advertisement from a man in Oregon looking for a wife. We corresponded for several weeks and he asked me to come out, sending the money for my trip. I spent weeks traveling by train and stagecoach to get here, arriving this morning to finally meet Duncan." Her chin quivered slightly, and she smiled.

"He was everything I'd hoped for. He seemed kind and caring and he'd been insistent that we get married immediately when I got off the coach. He took me to the church where I was able to get changed out of my dusty traveling clothes and Reverend Johnson performed the ceremony."

"Why did you agree to marry a man you'd never met? Were you running from something?"

He regretted the words the moment they were out of his mouth as he saw the anger flash in her eyes. She tipped her head slightly and squinted her eyes. "My reasons for marrying are none of your concern. I wanted a chance for a new life and the possibility for a family of my own. Why should my circumstances have anything to do with what happened to Duncan?"

Sighing loudly, he leaned forward to rest his

elbows on his knees. "Because I know the judge is going to want to know if you were coming out here with the intent to kill your new husband. I'm not trying to accuse you of anything and, perhaps, I could have worded my question a bit better but I do need to make sure we've covered everything before Judge Hargreaves gets here."

Their eyes held for a moment and he was sure if she could, she'd have told him exactly what she thought about him right then. Finally, she shrugged and turned her back to him, looking at the brick wall behind her. "I guess everyone will find out anyway, so I may as well tell you. My mother is what you might call a 'painted lady' who works in one of the classiest brothels in Jefferson City, Missouri. Well, at least that's what she says. Personally, since I grew up there, I have a different view of things. There is nothing classy about where she works or what she does."

He hated to think what she'd seen if she grew up in a brothel. He didn't want to ask her about her own involvement there but he knew it was something the judge would ask. However, before he could say anything, she turned back around and met his gaze.

"I know what you're thinking. No, I wasn't one of them. I managed to avoid it even though my mother kept trying to force me into that life. She wanted the extra income."

She went and sat on the edge of the cot, the loud squeaking of the old springs echoing against the walls. "Lucky for me, a kind doctor in town took pity on me and allowed me to work in his office, helping him clean and take care of things. The pay wasn't much but it was enough to keep my mother satisfied. As I got older, she was starting to become more insistent on me following the *family path* as she called it. When I saw Duncan's advertisement for a bride, I knew it was my chance to get away."

Her eyes had never wavered from his, as though she was daring him to judge her for the life she'd been born into.

"How old are you?"

"I'm seventeen. Usually by now, girls born into my life would have been working girls for at least four years. I've spent my last few years fighting to get away from that life and I knew if I didn't do something now, I wasn't going to be left with any other options."

She was the same age as Grace. His chest clenched as he tried to imagine his own sister having to deal with what this woman had endured. She was still so young and the thought of it angered him.

"You're free to believe what you want about me. But I am not like my mother. And I never killed Duncan. He was my one chance at happiness."

Her voice was filled with pain as she swallowed hard, clenching her hands together on her lap. Somehow, he knew she was telling the truth.

The hard part now was going to be proving it to everyone else. Just then, the door to his office swung open and a young man from town ran inside.

"Sheriff Hamilton, come quick! The church is on fire!"

CHAPTER 5

"Thank you, Grace, for allowing me a small bit of dignity."

Sylvia smiled warmly at the other woman, making sure the sheriff heard her. Hearing him sigh, she knew it had worked.

"Mrs. Coulter, I have apologized already for my lack of consideration to your needs. However, you have to understand, you're the first woman I've held behind the bars in this cell. The men who stay here are quite happy to use the small pot in the corner."

Thankfully, Grace had arrived early this morning, so Sylvia had been able to ask her for help. There was no way she was going to do her business in that small pot sitting out in the open for the whole world to see her.

"Well, unfortunately, my brother can be a bit thick-headed, so you'll have to forgive him for not realizing a woman would have different needs than the usual drunks he has locked up in here to keep him company."

Grace had escorted her to an outhouse in the back of the sheriff's office which truthfully wasn't much of a better option but at least it gave her some privacy. And since she was still a prisoner, the sheriff had been forced to stand at the back door to keep an eye on her in case she decided to escape.

She was sure she had to be completely exhausted because she almost had to laugh at how absurd the entire situation was.

"I've also brought you a new blouse and skirt you can wear. I'm sure they should fit you although you look like you could be a bit taller than me." Grace reached into a bag she'd brought and pulled out a pink blouse and cream-colored skirt. She turned and handed them to her.

"Thank you, Grace. I'm glad to have a friend here."

Grace turned and glared at her brother. "Now, Luke, would it be all right if I take Sylvia up to your room and let her change her clothes with some privacy?"

Sylvia almost laughed at the exasperated look on the sheriff's face.

"Grace, I don't know why you're so angry with me. I'm just doing my job. I can't be held personally responsible for the fact there are no cells designed just for women. The best I can do is possibly find a curtain to hang in the corner to give her some privacy for changing."

"Well, I hope you don't expect her to use that pot behind some curtain. There are some things a woman shouldn't have to do and one of those is doing her business out in the open with nothing more than a cloth protecting her."

The sheriff looked at Sylvia and once again she found her heart skipping a beat at the brightness of those eyes. She honestly wondered if he could read her mind.

"No, I wouldn't expect that. I'll make sure she gets out whenever she needs to go."

Sylvia's cheeks burned as everyone sat discussing her personal needs like they were talking about the weather.

The sheriff thrust his hand through his hair as he leaned forward and placed his elbows onto his desk. He still had dirt and soot on his face from spending the night with the other townsfolk fighting the fire at the church. She'd been able to hear the commotion outside and had peeked out the small window in her cell to see the flames that had seemed to be reaching for the sky. She knew he hadn't slept and had come straight back here to make sure she was all right.

Since he hadn't forced her to get back inside the cell yet, she sat on the chair next to his desk, placing the clothes Grace had given her onto her lap. "So, were you able to save any of the church?"

He shook his head as his gaze found hers. "I'm afraid not. Everything's gone. Thankfully Reverend Johnson had gone to the boardinghouse for supper, so wasn't in his small apartment in the basement. I doubt he'd have been able to get out once the fire started."

"Do they know what caused it?" Grace sat down in the chair across from the desk, obviously finished chastising her brother for now.

"I'm going to go take a look around today to see if I can find any clues but it's hard to say. Could have been a candle left going or a lantern tipping over."

"With the church gone, all of the paperwork for my marriage will be gone too." She hated to bring up her own personal issues knowing how hard it would be for the town having just lost something so special to them all. But right now, she needed to figure out how to keep herself from hanging.

But the sheriff had obviously been thinking the same thing as he nodded. "I'm afraid so. All records are gone."

She clenched her teeth tightly and swallowed the lump in her throat. Now as far as anyone was concerned, her marriage might not have even happened. Nothing would have been sent off yet.

"It doesn't matter. I don't want any of his money or anything anyway. But it would have been nice to at least be able to prove that he'd trusted me enough to make me his wife. And that I wasn't just coming here for his money."

The sheriff was watching her closely. "Well, the Reverend will be able to vouch for your marriage. It should be enough for the judge. And if you can prove you didn't kill Duncan, you'll be entitled to everything as his wife."

She met his eyes. "I don't want his money even if I do win. There will always be doubt in people's minds about my innocence if I take it."

Grace looked at her with her mouth hanging open. "Sylvia, I have no doubt in my mind about your innocence and I've only just met you." She turned and widened her eyes at her brother. "And

Luke is going to prove it so that no one else has any doubts either."

Luke looked at his sister, then closed his eyes briefly. She could see how tired he was. "If she's innocent, I will do everything I can to prove it."

Sylvia realized that even though Grace believed her, the sheriff was still not entirely convinced. She tried to ignore the flicker of pain that rushed through her stomach. She knew he was the sheriff, so he had to listen to all sides and make his decisions based on facts. Since she didn't have any way to prove she was innocent, she couldn't blame him for not completely believing her.

She was just going to have to try harder to make sure he did.

Grace stood up and put her hand out for hers. "Now, I'm going to take Sylvia up to your room to let her get cleaned up and changed into more suitable clothes. Then I will come sit down here with her and keep her company today while you catch some sleep."

The sheriff was looking at his sister with his mouth gaping. Finally, he turned and shook his head in her direction.

"Well, it looks like the boss has spoken. I'm

sure glad to have a witness around to see what I have to put up with."

Sylvia smiled and shrugged. "I'm just glad to have her on my side. Even if no one else believes me."

A shadow crossed his face and he nodded slowly.

"I'll let Grace help you but I'm afraid I'll have to return you to the cell when you get back down. If Randolph or his mother show up and sees you sitting out here, there'll be hell to pay."

Holding herself stiffly, she followed Grace toward the stairs leading up to the sheriff's room.

"Of course. You have to follow the law."

She didn't know why she was angry with him for doing his job. But for some reason, it hurt knowing he didn't believe her.

And how could she prove otherwise when she was stuck behind bars?

CHAPTER 6

There was a hushed silence as the people of Bethany stood around the remains of the church. Some of them were picking through the ashes to see if there were any remnants of their beloved building remaining.

The church had been one of the first buildings put up when Bethany was founded and every resident standing there had spent their Sundays inside these walls. Many of them had been married inside or had their children baptized.

"I just can't see what could have caused it. Reverend Johnson is sure he didn't leave a lantern or candle going anywhere." Colton Wallace, who was married to Luke's other sister Phoebe, was reaching down and moving aside some of the rubble. He'd been friends with Colton for years and when he'd ended up marrying his sister, Luke had been thrilled.

"Well, Reverend Johnson is getting a bit old. Perhaps he's just forgotten." Colton's brother Reid was beside them as they searched for clues.

They all knew the Reverend had been forgetting a great deal these days, so it really wasn't a stretch that he might have forgotten he'd left a candle burning. But Luke had a niggling feeling he couldn't seem to shake. He just wasn't convinced this was an accident.

The smell of smoke still hung heavy in the air and he knew the hearts of everyone standing around were likely aching with the pain of what had happened. The mood was somber and some of the women were crying while their husbands held them. He was sure every man in Bethany had spent the night out here alongside their neighbors trying to save this small church and, as he looked around, he could see the defeated looks in everyone's eyes.

Just then, James O'Hara, the man who'd come west with the Wallace family many years ago and was one of the founding citizens of Bethany stood up in front of the crowd. "We lost an important piece of our history last night but that doesn't mean we need to lose hope. We are a strong community who have helped rebuild barns after fire. We've joined together to help others in times of sickness and we've all worked together to build this small town into a place where future generations can be proud to live."

Everyone was listening as James spoke. "We'll rebuild this church and use this as a chance to show the strength of the people of our town."

The people gathered around started to clap and cheer. Luke was thankful James had managed to turn the mood around because, right now, he had his own worries to deal with. If he couldn't find any evidence that the church was deliberately burned down, then all his suspicions would be nothing more than that. Without proof, he wasn't sure how he could help the woman back in his jail cell.

The timing just seemed to be too coincidental for Luke. But he couldn't be sure he wasn't just letting his dislike for Randolph cloud his thinking. Surely the man wouldn't have stooped so low as to burn the church, would he?

Luke suspected that Randolph didn't want Sylvia getting any of his brother's money and he could understand the man's feelings. If he'd found out his brother had just been murdered by a new wife who would now be getting everything, Luke knew he'd be just as angry.

But would he go so far as to burn down the church to get rid of any evidence of the marriage happening?

"So, Grace tells me you've got some excitement happening here in town. Do you have any clues about what happened to Duncan Coulter?" Colton kept digging while he spoke.

"Just that his brother Randolph dragged the man's poor new wife into town tied up in the back of his wagon like a pig going to slaughter."

Colton lifted his head and looked at him with an eyebrow raised. "What makes him think she did it? Grace says she's certain the woman didn't do anything."

"When Randolph found them, she was apparently leaning over Duncan holding a rock with blood on it. And he's certain she only came here for the money she could get when her husband was out of the way."

Colton squinted his eyebrows together. "That sounds a bit far-fetched to me. Unless she's a woman bigger than us, I doubt she'd have the strength to kill a man Duncan's size."

Luke just nodded. He'd thought the same thing but, without any proof, it was Randolph's word against hers. And no one knew her around here, so it was going to be harder for her to prove her case.

"So, what do you think?" Both Colton and Reid were looking at him with interest.

He just shrugged and shook his head. "I honestly have no idea. I want to believe her but, as the sheriff, it's up to me to make sure I find out the truth. When she came in, she was covered in blood and her blouse was torn up. She says it was from struggling with Randolph as he dragged her into the wagon but what if she's lying?"

Reid leaned on a shovel he'd been using to move debris around. "What if she's not? You need to help her if she is telling the truth. You don't want that on your shoulders knowing you've let an innocent woman be charged with something she didn't do."

Clenching his jaw tightly, Luke stood and looked back toward his office. He'd asked Grace to stay with her again so she wouldn't be left by herself.

"You know, when I took this job as sheriff, I assumed I'd be doing nothing more than breaking up a few fights in the saloon and hauling the odd drunk into the cell to sleep it off until morning. I never thought I'd be left in charge of proving a woman's innocence, when I have no way of knowing if she's guilty or not. If I get it wrong, it won't be fair to anyone involved."

"Well, I've come to realize that the people in your family are generally pretty good at seeing the truth in people. So I'd trust what Grace believes. And I'd trust your own gut. The people of Bethany wouldn't have hired you as sheriff if they didn't believe you were fair or that you couldn't do the job."

Luke appreciated his friend's trust in him but it didn't make things any easier. He'd already sent a message to the judge, so he knew he only had a few days to figure things out. Once Sylvia was taken from here, there'd be nothing he could do to help her.

If she was innocent, he had to hurry and figure out how to prove it.

CHAPTER 7

Grace had already gone home, leaving her alone with the sheriff in the quickly fading light of the day. He'd lit a lantern and was now sitting at his desk doing some paperwork.

"I really am sorry to have caused so much trouble." She gave a sharp laugh. "Here I thought by now, I'd be spending my first few days as a married woman, getting to know my new husband, but, instead, I'm spending my time with the local sheriff."

He lifted his head and raised an eyebrow. "To be fair, I can think of worse people you could be stuck spending your time with."

When he smiled, his eyes seemed even brighter, which she wouldn't have thought possible.

She laughed quietly. "I supposed you're right. I should be thankful the sheriff here isn't an old codger who wouldn't be willing to at least listen to a woman when she tries to give her side of the story."

He leaned back in his chair and stretched. "I'm glad to hear you don't think I'm an old codger."

The room was quiet but outside the open window at the front, she could hear the sounds of the town going on around them. A wagon bounced down the street, the wooden floorboards squeaking with every bump. Everyone else was just going about their lives without a care in the world, while she was sitting in here waiting to find out her fate.

It wasn't fair but then not much in her life had been fair up until this point anyway. And she'd always somehow managed to get through it.

She could get through this too.

"Do you think I'll hang if the judge finds me guilty?" Speaking the worries out loud sent her pulse racing. She'd tried not to let the thoughts make their way into her head, but they kept winning.

The sheriff didn't move, holding her eyes in his gaze. A clock ticking was the only sound in the room as she waited for him to answer. Finally, he shook his head slowly. "I'm going to do my best to make sure that doesn't happen."

"Why would you do that for me? Don't you think I should pay if I did murder my husband?"

He crossed his arms in front of him as he leaned back in his chair. "If you did murder your husband, then I believe you should pay but not with your life."

She sat down on the edge of her cot, the springs squeaking loudly. "How are you going to prove I didn't do it? No one is going to believe me."

Once more, he watched her without moving. "Well, lucky for you, I believe you. I don't know how I'll prove it but I will."

An unfamiliar feeling hit her in the stomach as she realized for the first time in her life she had someone on her side. She had to put her faith in him and hope he could prove her innocence.

She looked past him and through the window across the room. Stars were shining bright in the skies beyond the buildings she could see. She wished she could go outside and feel the cool breeze of the night air against her skin. She dreaded the thought of spending the night alone in this cell again, knowing if she needed anything she'd be on her own. Last night Luke had been fighting the fire at the church but she'd at least known he was around and awake if she'd needed him.

"Will you be able to hear me calling if I need something during the night?"

He nodded. "I will. I'll leave my door open so if you are in need of anything, you only need to yell."

They sat quietly listening to the minutes tick by on the clock. Finally, he stood up and walked over to the cell. "I wish there was some other way to do this and I didn't have to hold you in here. But I have to follow the law."

She smiled and nodded. "I know. I wouldn't expect you to do anything that could put your job at risk."

"I've got some warmer blankets upstairs that I'll bring down for you. I know the cot isn't very comfortable but I hope you can at least get some sleep."

"I'll be fine. I've slept on worse." She appreciated his consideration and was once again thankful she'd been left in his care. There were many lawmen who wouldn't be so willing to try making things more comfortable for her.

"I'm sorry I wasn't able to get your things

from Randolph. But I know Grace will be more than happy to give you some more clothes and anything else you need. Once everything is over, Randolph will have to give you back your items whether he likes it or not."

She knew he'd sent someone out to the farm to get her things this morning but Randolph had refused to send them to her, saying she was a criminal and he was holding onto them as evidence. She didn't know what kind of evidence he thought he'd find but she didn't really care. The two small bags she'd brought west with her didn't have much of value anyway.

"So, what will you do when you get out? Will you go back to Missouri?"

She shrugged. "I really don't know. I don't think I'll go back but I don't know what other options I have. It's not like I have the money to go back or any reason to for that matter."

He stood up and stretched again. He was a tall man, with dark hair that seemed in such contrast compared to the brightness of his eyes. His shoulders were wide under the leather vest he wore and as he twisted, the buttons on his shirt pulled with the muscle underneath.

What was wrong with her? She was in jail, waiting to find out if she'd hang for the murder of her new husband and here she was getting all agog over the man holding her prisoner.

She was, obviously, overtired and rattled from everything that had happened over the past twenty-four hours.

"Well, it's going to be a long day tomorrow. I'm going out to Duncan's farm to see what I can find out. I'm not happy about having to see Randolph and listen to him tell me what I'm doing wrong but I have to do it. Hopefully now that the shock of what happened has worn off, it'll be easier to get a statement from him."

Nodding, she clenched her jaw tight. "He'll tell you the same thing. He came along and I was leaning over Duncan, holding the rock covered with blood. But I was only holding it because I'd found it lying beside his body. I swear I never hit him with it."

He came over next to the cell. "I know."

"How do you know?"

He shrugged. "I just do. So leave the worrying up to me and try to get some sleep. Grace will be by first thing in the morning and I've asked Mrs. Larsen to come with your breakfast. It might not be a luxurious hotel you're staying in, but I'll do my best to at least make sure you're comfortable."

"Thank you."

The words didn't seem to be enough to show her gratitude for his help. But right now, there was nothing else she could say. She was relying on a total stranger to keep her from hanging but, thankfully, the man was willing to do everything he could to help her.

CHAPTER 8

Cursing loudly, he slammed the piece of paper down on his desk. Grace dropped the wash basin she'd been carrying, splashing water all over the ground. She whipped around and glared at him. "Luke Hamilton! Watch your mouth!"

"I'm sorry. I'm not used to having so many women hanging around my office." He thrust his fingers through his hair in frustration. Standing up, he went over and crouched down beside his sister to help her clean up the mess.

"Well, what was on the paper that was dropped off? Whatever it was must not be good."

He shook his head, quickly glancing over toward the woman in the cell. She'd just washed up and now that the last of the dried blood had finally been removed from her cuts, her bruises seemed even darker.

Every time he looked at her with the split on her lip, the one by her eye and the many bruises that were marring her skin, anger would coil in his stomach. No one should have had to endure what she did at the hands of Randolph. Luke understood the anger he'd been feeling at the sight of his brother lying dead but it was no excuse for his behavior toward a woman.

If he didn't know it would just make the man even more trouble to deal with, Luke would be charging him with assault.

"It would appear that Randolph has contacted the judge himself and is demanding action immediately. Judge Hargreaves will now be here in two days' time, so we won't have as much time to figure everything out." He kept his eyes on hers as he continued. "And it seems that the judge will be escorting Mrs. Coulter to Oregon City right away to face trial."

Grace gasped but Sylvia just stood perfectly still. Finally, she leaned her head onto the bars of the cell, her hands gripped tightly around the metal.

"So, I won't be able to have my case heard by the judge here? No one in Oregon City even knows me."

Standing back up, he walked over by her cell. "I still have a couple of days before the judge gets here. Don't give up just yet."

She lifted her eyes to his, suddenly flashing with anger. "Do you know how hard it is to just sit here while my fate is left in everyone else's hands? I can't do anything to help. You keep telling me not to worry but you have no idea how this feels."

"You're right, I don't know how it feels. But you have to trust me. I'm not going to just let the judge drag you away from here without giving you a fighting chance."

She turned her back to him, wrapping her arms around herself. "I don't have any choice, do I? I'll sit here while a bunch of men decide if I hang or if I can go free. And I know how men work. They'll want justice against a woman who they believe has done an atrocity to her husband, the man she's supposed to be obedient to." She turned back to face him and shook her head. "No, I know exactly what my fate will be."

Grace came over and stood beside him. "You

know she didn't do it and I know she didn't do it. So why don't you just let her go before the judge gets here?"

He sighed loudly and went to grab his hat from the hook. "You know I can't do that, Grace. Just keep an eye on her while I go out to Duncan's to speak to Randolph."

He was just as angry as Sylvia. He didn't appreciate the other man going behind his back to contact the judge after he'd already sent the message. Now he had to work fast or the woman in his jail cell was going to pay for a crime she didn't commit. Because even though he would never admit it, Luke agreed with everything she'd just said.

She wouldn't be given a fair chance. He'd seen enough of how the law around here worked to know that as a woman, you didn't have the same rights as a man.

So it was up to him to give her a fighting chance.

"OH, you poor thing. What kind of monster could do this to someone as pretty as you?" Sylvia smiled at the woman who'd walked over to her cell. She'd heard her come through the door, then speak with Grace.

"Sylvia, this is Susan O'Hara. She runs the mercantile in town with her husband, James. Susan, this is Sylvia Coulter."

"Well, it's nice to meet you, Mrs. Coulter. Grace has told me all about you, and I must say I'm shocked to see the injuries you've suffered at the hands of your husband's brother. Honestly, in all my days..." The older woman brought her hand up to her chest and shook her head in disgust.

"I'm all right, Mrs. O'Hara. The sheriff and Grace have both been taking good care of me here."

"Don't you dare call me Mrs. O'Hara! Everyone calls me Susan and that's the only thing I'll answer to. Now you come sit out here with us, so we can share this cake I've made."

Susan was already moving around and pulling food out of a bag she'd set on the sheriff's desk. "Grace, you put some tea on. I know Luke has a kettle in here somewhere."

Sylvia looked over at Grace in stunned silence, and her friend just grinned and shrugged. "But I can't come out, Mrs.—I mean, Susan. And please called me Sylvia. Sheriff Hamilton has said I'm only allowed out when I need to take care of my personal needs, and then Grace has to escort me outside."

Susan looked up and scowled. "Well, Luke won't mind. I'll take the blame. Grace, you let her out of that miserable cell so the poor thing can come sit on a nice, comfortable chair and enjoy some company."

"Aren't you afraid I'll try to escape?"

Susan just laughed. "Oh, heavens no. Who would want to escape and miss out on having a piece of cake?"

Sylvia had to smile. "That's true. I would never turn down any delicious baking."

Grace opened her cell and for a brief moment, Sylvia hesitated, knowing the sheriff would most likely be angry if he caught her out of the cell enjoying a tea party in his office. But then she figured she really didn't have anything to lose. If this was the one chance she'd have for a break from a jail cell, then she was going to take it.

Walking out, she went over and took the chair being offered by Susan. "You sit down here and get comfortable. I want you to tell me everything that's happened."

Taking the wedge of chocolate cake being

offered to her, she looked at Susan in disbelief. "You know I'm in here because it's believed I killed my new husband, Duncan Coulter, right?"

Susan sliced a piece of the cake and handed it over to Grace. "Of course, I know that. Everyone in town is talking about it. Randolph has been spewing his accusations to everyone who will listen which, truthfully, isn't many people. The man isn't well liked around these parts." She put a piece onto a plate and sat down in the chair across from Sylvia. "But I like to hear things for myself before I make my decision on what I'll believe or not."

After Sylvia had some time to get over her shock at the kindness of the other woman, she started to speak and, before she knew it, she'd told her everything from the past few days and even back into her childhood. Susan had a way of making you feel like she genuinely cared when you were talking to her and Sylvia just couldn't seem to stop herself.

With tears forming in her eyes, she told about finding Duncan and how scared she'd been as she was dragged into Randolph's wagon. Susan reached out and placed her hand over hers, giving her the strength to finish what she was saying.

"But thankfully, Sheriff Hamilton seems to be

on my side and wants to help me prove my innocence. If he hadn't believed me, I'm not sure where I'd be right now."

Susan was nodding as she patted her hand. "Yes, you are lucky to be in Luke's care. He's the most fair and honest man I know, so don't you worry. He'll help you and he won't stop until he has. That's just who he is. And that's why this town voted to have him elected as sheriff."

"Except now the judge is coming back to town early, so we don't have much time. I'm worried there isn't anything Luke will be able to do to help Sylvia." Grace looked over at her and smiled sadly.

"Oh, I'm sure Luke won't let them take her when there's a chance she's innocent."

"There's not much he can do. If the judge gets here before he can find any proof, Sylvia will be taken to Oregon City and there won't be anything we can do to help her."

Hearing her friend say it out loud sent her heart plummeting to the pit of her stomach. She tried to smile as she brought her tea cup to her lips with trembling hands. "I'm sure everything will work out. Now, do you think I could have another piece of your wonderful cake, Susan? I haven't tasted anything so delicious in a very long time."

"Of course, dear. And don't you worry. I know Luke Hamilton and he won't rest until he's cleared your name and set you free."

CHAPTER 9

She looked up at the shadows flickering along the ceiling in the bright moonlight. The blanket was pulled up tight to her neck as she tried to keep the chill away. Every sound outside the window made her heart jump and the constant ticking of the clock counting down the minutes until the judge would arrive was keeping her awake.

Sheriff Hamilton had spent the past two days tirelessly going through all the statements and repeatedly asking her questions about everything that had happened. He'd been out to Duncan's but Randolph had become enraged that he wasn't just accepting his word that Sylvia had killed his brother. He wouldn't let the sheriff look around the property, other than showing him the spot where he'd found her leaning over Duncan.

But now her time was up. The judge had sent word today that he would arrive in the morning. Every time she thought about what was going to happen to her, she struggled to breathe.

Taking a deep breath, she rolled over and looked out the window on the far side of the room onto the street as she pulled the blanket tightly around herself. In the corner, Luke's hat and jacket hung on the hook. When she closed her eyes briefly, she saw those eyes in her mind.

After spending the past few days in this small room with Sheriff Hamilton, she'd come to know him well. He'd been kind and had made sure she had everything she needed. He'd asked Mrs. Larsen from the boardinghouse in town to bring her meals each day and he'd even let her out of her cell to eat at the desk with him.

She was sure that wasn't something most prisoners would be allowed to do.

But then, she was quickly realizing that Sheriff Hamilton was a lot different than most men and that included other lawmen she'd known in her life.

Suddenly, her eyes spotted something move by

the desk. Surely her eyes were just playing tricks on her.

Squinting, she tried to get a better look by sitting up and leaning out slightly. It must have just been a piece of paper falling on the floor or something.

Just as she was about to lie back down, it moved again and ran straight at her. Screaming in terror, she jumped up to her feet, standing on the cot as she hugged the blanket to her.

The mouse stopped and stared at her before running toward her again. She'd never imagined herself to be the type of girl to jump screaming at a mouse but being alone in this cell with no way to get out was distorting her senses.

"What's wrong?"

Sheriff Hamilton raced into the room from the stairway with his gun drawn. His hair was disheveled from sleep, and her cheeks burned as she realized he'd only pulled his pants on, not even buttoning them up. His shoulders and chest were bare, and as he ran over to her cell, she had to force herself to stop staring.

He unlocked her cell and quickly came inside, looking all around to see what had scared her. "What happened? Are you all right?"

He put his hand out for her and she took it,

feeling the warmth of his fingers in hers as he helped her step down. Her cheeks were burning even more now when she realized she was going to have to tell him what had happened.

"Well, you can likely put your gun away. I'm afraid I was just startled by a mouse and might have over-reacted."

She didn't even want to look him in the eye, so she kept her gaze down on the floor. When she heard him snicker, she lifted her eyes and offered him an apologetic smile. "I'm sorry to have woken you. I'm normally not so skittish around small rodents but being in such a tight space with no way of escape might have caused me to scare a little easier."

His mouth was pulled tight as he looked like he fought the laughter threatening to escape.

She shrugged and laughed softly. "You're free to laugh. I can admit when I've done something a bit silly."

Finally, he laughed loudly and shook his head in disbelief. "I was sure someone was down here trying to kill you the way you screamed. I was afraid of what I was going to find when I got here."

She laughed with him, letting the anxiety and worry of the past few days lift from her shoulders for a few moments. He went and set his gun on the desk as he shook with laughter. When he could finally speak again, he turned back to face her, crossing his arms over his chest while he leaned back on the edge of his desk.

"That's just Squeak."

When she looked at him with her eyebrows pulled together, he laughed again. "The mouse. My two-year old niece was here one day and saw him. That was one of the only words she could say as she clapped when she saw him. So we called him Squeak and he lives here in peace with me."

Sylvia had walked to the edge of her cell, not going outside the open door. She still held the blanket tightly around her, even though she'd been sleeping in her clothes. The last thing she wanted was someone walking in while she was in a nightgown and since this was a public place, she wasn't taking that risk.

Trying to keep her eyes from straying to his bare chest, she nervously looked around for any sign of Squeak anywhere. While she really wasn't afraid of mice, the thought of the small critter running around while she slept did make her uneasy.

He must have realized he was standing there half-naked, so he finally went and grabbed a shirt that had been hanging by the small stove in the other corner. Throwing it over his shoulders, he kept his back to her as he looked down and did up the buttons. She watched the muscles in his back moving as his hands worked.

When he turned around, her skin burned with embarrassment. He'd caught her looking and was now standing with his head tipped slightly to one side and an eyebrow raised. He was slowly rolling the sleeves up.

"Um...I didn't realize you had a niece. I know Grace hasn't mentioned being married so I assume you must have another brother or sister." Her voice was shaky as she tried to cover her embarrassment.

She moved over to sit on the small chair in her cell.

"You can come sit out here where it's a bit warmer. I'm not afraid of you escaping in the dark, especially when I know now that you're afraid of a little mouse."

She looked at him in shock, then rolled her eyes as she saw the grin on his face and realized he was joking with her.

Coming out to sit in the more comfortable chair by the stove, she laughed. "I told you I'm not afraid of a mouse. I was just startled, that's all."

He went and lit a lantern on his desk, then pulled his chair out to sit across from her. The soft glow of the light flickered between them, letting her see those eyes that seemed to see right into her soul.

"My other sister, Phoebe. She married my longtime friend, Colton Wallace. His family owns a large area of land that they farm here in Bethany. They have twins—Robert and Laura. They're a bit of a handful and I'm afraid Laura might have her uncle Luke wrapped around her little finger."

He was leaning forward, resting his elbows on his legs as he spoke.

"So, do you have any more family? What about your parents?" She was enjoying this moment of peacefulness before everything that would happen tomorrow, and she didn't want it to end.

He kept his gaze on the floor in front of him. "My parents are both gone. My ma died from cholera back home in St. Louis. Not long after, my pa was killed in a fire in our shop. I wasn't around because I'd had a bit of a falling out with him and didn't want to be stuck in the family business. I was sure I could find my fortune elsewhere and had taken off, leaving Phoebe and Grace alone."

His voice was filled with pain as he spoke about his past. "I'm so sorry, Sheriff. I didn't know."

He lifted his eyes to hers and shrugged. "You couldn't have known. And please, stop calling me sheriff. That's not my name. Call me Luke."

"I will but only if you stop calling me Mrs. Coulter. I don't feel like it's fair for me to use Duncan's name when we were only married for such a short time. Just call me Sylvia."

"I don't think Duncan would be opposed to you using his name. But if you'd prefer, Sylvia, that's what I'll use."

Her stomach did a strange twist as she heard her name come from his lips. She was sure he wasn't going to continue telling her any more about what had happened with his parents. But finally, he leaned back and continued. "My sisters were left in the care of my uncle Ivan who wasn't a good man. By the time I got back, it was too late to make amends with my pa. And Phoebe had some concerns that Ivan might have been responsible for the death of my father, so I got them both as far away from him as I could. That's how they ended up out here. I put them on a wagon train coming west with Colton and I went back to St. Louis to find out the truth."

She listened breathlessly. "So, did you?"

He shook his head angrily. "No, there wasn't any way to prove what we suspected. It took me some time to get over the anger at him for what I know he did and at myself for not being there for my sisters when they needed me. I'd been selfish for too long, so that's why I eventually ended up in Bethany, determined to settle down and start my life here. I owe that to them."

"Sheriff...I mean, Luke, I'm sure your sisters don't hold any anger toward you. You can't blame yourself. Although I'd say by how much Grace hangs out around here, that she's quite happy that you've chosen to stay around."

He laughed. "Yes, she does tend to be under my feet quite a bit but I don't mind. She was only twelve when our parents died and other than Phoebe and Colton, I'm the only family she has." He smiled over at her. "Although I think she's hanging around even more since you showed up. There aren't many other women her age around here for her to be friends with."

She hugged her arms tighter to her chest and sighed. "I am so glad to have her but I hope she won't end up being too upset when I leave in the morning. She's done so much to help me and I just don't want her to feel like she's let me down in any way."

The silence of the room surrounded them, and the familiar ticking of the clock seemed to echo even louder.

"I'm not going to let them take you."

"Luke, we both know there's nothing you can do. I'm just going to have to hope I get a judge who is fair and maybe he'll believe me."

"Sylvia, I'm going to need you to trust me. I won't let you pay for a crime you didn't commit."

She kept her eyes on his, not sure what to say. How could he keep her from leaving tomorrow?

He couldn't and she knew it.

CHAPTER 10

"So, what's your plan? You're not just going to let this judge haul her off to face trial in Oregon City, are you?"

Luke moved a board away from the rubble of the church and pulled it to the side where they were piling the mess to be hauled away. He was still hoping to find something that could give him some answers about the fire but so far there hadn't been anything. He'd needed something to get his mind off of what was happening today, so he'd come out early to help some of the men from town with the clean-up.

Titus Caine stood watching him while he waited for Luke to answer. Titus was married to Colton's twin sister Ella and had come in to help at the church this morning for a bit after picking up some feed for his horses.

"Why is everyone in my family so concerned with this woman I have locked up?"

He knew he was being grumpy but the worry of the past few days had caught up to him. And knowing the judge would be here within the next few hours had him on edge. He'd run out of time to find the evidence he needed to help her.

Titus grinned and bent down to pick a piece of debris up, quickly throwing it to the side. "Well, according to Grace, that woman you have locked up is innocent. And as you know, I've had my share of people believing the worst about me without knowing the whole story. So, I'd say if she *is* innocent, then someone better be doing something to help her."

When Titus had first come to town, he'd lied about who he was to try and find out who had killed his brother. He'd been angry and hadn't gone out of his way to make many friends. But as they'd gotten to know him, everyone had realized he wasn't what they'd all believed him to be.

"I'm trying. But I'm sure if anyone would understand how hard it can be to find the proof you need, it would be you. And Randolph doesn't make it any easier. He's so angry that he won't even listen to reason. He's insisting she pay for killing his brother."

Titus nodded. "I can understand his anger. He's only doing what he thinks has to be done to get justice for his brother."

Luke scowled, knowing Titus was right. But that didn't make it any easier.

Suddenly, he heard his name being called from down the street. Turning, he saw Grace running toward him. "Luke, I'm so sorry! I just turned my head for a second and she was gone."

"What do you mean, she was gone?"

He raced toward his office, knowing already what he was going to find. Throwing the door open, he ran inside and saw the empty cell. Quickly turning, he almost collided with Grace who'd run in behind him. "Where is she?"

"I took her outside to use the outhouse and I thought I heard someone calling me from inside. I quickly came back in to check and when I got back out, she was gone."

Titus came in behind them and whistled loudly. "Well, she's definitely not the type of woman to sit around and wait for her fate to be handed to her. I like her already." He was grinning at Luke, who rolled his eyes and turned his back on the man.

While he was trying to figure out what to do next, the man he'd known was coming, walked through the door. Judge Hargreaves stopped and looked around in confusion at everyone standing in the room. "Well, I wasn't expecting a welcome party, Sheriff."

Groaning to himself, Luke went over to shake the man's hand. He was a fair judge but he wasn't going to be happy to hear he'd come all this way earlier than expected and the prisoner he was supposed to escort to Oregon City had just escaped.

"It's good to see you, Judge. But I'm afraid there's a bit of a problem and you're not going to be happy about it."

SHE PUT her head in her hands and tried to stop her body from shaking. She wasn't sure if it was from fear, cold or exhaustion, but all she knew was ever since she'd stopped running, her body had been trembling. There was a thick blanket folded up in the far corner of the cave where she was hiding.

What had she done?

Now, she'd likely made Grace get into trouble. And Luke could lose his job.

She should have never agreed to this.

"Sylvia, are you all right?"

Just as she began to feel like the cave walls were collapsing in around her, the sound of Grace's voice was like a hand reaching out to comfort her.

"I'm back here, Grace." She crawled out to the opening, standing up when the warm air hit her skin. "It's so chilly inside there but I know it will work well to keep me hidden." She pulled her friend into her arms and hugged her tight. "Thank you so much for doing this. But I'm worried we've made a big mistake. If they find me now, they will believe I'm guilty, just because I ran. And I could get you and Luke into so much trouble if they find out the truth."

She pulled away from her friend and started pacing around the open spot among the trees. Grace had explained exactly where to go. She'd gone along and left small pieces of orange fabric tied to branches to help lead her to the cave where she could hide.

The sound of birds singing around her helped to calm her nerves and just being outside in the fresh air was like a balm to her soul. After being locked up for days inside that small cell, sleeping next to Squeak the mouse, she was just happy to be out where the world was alive around her.

There was a slight breeze and it picked her hair up and blew some stray pieces over her eyes. Pushing it back, she went and sat on a stump beside the cave opening. Grace came and sat beside her.

"I knew the risks when Luke mentioned it to me. And he knows the risks too. But he's too honorable to let a woman pay for a crime when he knows she's innocent. He wasn't going to let them take you, knowing if he can just have a bit more time, he can find what he needs to clear your name.

"But now that I've escaped, I can't ever go back if he doesn't find the proof he needs. I will spend the rest of my life on the run."

Grace nodded slowly and gave her a sad smile. "I know. But I also know my brother won't quit until he proves your innocence. So we need to just trust him and believe he'll make things right, somehow."

She stared at her friend for a while, wondering how she could have gotten so lucky to have this woman on her side. And her brother. Luke didn't have to believe her and he sure didn't have to risk his job to help her. But he had and she wasn't going to betray his trust. He'd given her a chance by staying here until he had the proof he needed, knowing there was a chance she would keep running.

She wouldn't do that to him. She could have been long gone by now but she knew that if she did, no one would ever be able to trust her again. And she couldn't have lived with herself.

So, she would stay here and pray that Luke knew what he was doing.

CHAPTER 11

"What do you mean she escaped? How could you have let this happen?" Randolph's voice filled the room, his anger evident by the redness of his face and the veins standing out on his neck. "I knew you were getting soft on that woman and now look what's happened."

The man turned to face the judge. "I want him arrested. And his sister because I have no doubt they were in cahoots to let this murderer go."

Judge Hargreaves was sitting back, quietly watching the exchange. Randolph had come in hoping to see the judge cart Sylvia off to Oregon City but had instead been met with the news of her escape.

He wasn't happy.

Titus had left, so now he was alone with Randolph and the judge. The door to the empty cell stood wide open, seeming to cause Randolph even more rage every time he looked in that direction.

"Someone had to have opened that cell for her to get out. I know she's a murderer but I doubt she'd have the ability to pick a lock."

Luke sighed, once more repeating everything he could to try explaining it all to the man. "I've already told you this a hundred times. Grace was in charge of escorting Sylvia to the facilities in the back during the day. It was the only way to give the woman some semblance of privacy."

"See! He's even using her name...Sylvia! That sounds a bit too familiar for a sheriff to be calling his prisoner by her first name."

Luke glared at the man. He was leaning against his desk, with his arms crossed over his chest. Clenching his fists that were folded under his arms, he spoke much more calmly than what was raging inside him.

"*Mrs. Coulter* has spent the past few days locked in this small room with me. I've had the chance to get to know her and to know the truth about her character. She asked me to call her by her given name and I've honored that request. I'm sorry you don't feel that is appropriate, however, I do things based on my own gut instincts, not by what someone else is telling me is wrong."

"Well, what are you going to do now, Sheriff? Are you just going to let her get away since you seem to know so much about her character? You seem to be swayed by a pretty face, however, I was the one who saw her holding the rock that killed my brother. That's a fact that can't be denied."

Luke was shaking with anger. "*Pretty face?* You mean the one that was covered in scratches and bruises when she showed up here, after being dragged on the ground and tossed into the wagon to be brought in?" He stood and slowly walked over to Randolph. "I'm only swayed by the truth and I have no doubt in my mind that the woman you roughed up and accused of murder is innocent. And, in fact, was just as distraught at finding her dead husband as you were."

Randolph glared at him, with neither of them moving as they stood toe-to-toe.

Finally, Judge Hargreaves pushed his chair back with a loud scraping sound across the floor. "Listen to me, I think we all need to discuss this when our heads have a chance to cool down. We aren't solving anything by this. Randolph, I'm sure Sheriff Hamilton will do everything he can to find the escaped prisoner. So for now, take yourself home and let us handle things."

Luke never moved and Randolph squinted at him in anger and shook his head before turning and slamming the office door behind him.

"So, Luke, do you want to tell me exactly what happened? And where your sister is now?"

Closing his eyes briefly, Luke took a moment to gather his thoughts and get his emotions back under control before turning to face the judge. He knew the man was going to have questions, so he better be prepared to answer.

He hated lying and he knew what he was doing was wrong but he'd been left with no other choice.

He just hoped he hadn't made a huge mistake.

THE SUN HAD GONE DOWN over the horizon, leaving her cloaked in darkness. Stars filled the sky above her as she sat wrapped in her blanket. She was desperately trying to keep her heart from racing with every sound she heard around her but she knew there was no way she'd be able to sleep at all tonight.

While the cave offered her protection from the weather, should it rain or be cold, it didn't do much to keep any wild animals from coming inside. Thankfully, Grace had made sure she had a lantern to take in the cave with her and right now she had a fire burning right near the opening. Hopefully, it would be enough to scare any animals away.

She put her hands out to warm them over the fire, then jumped as she heard a branch snapping just on the other side of the trees. Scared to move, she scanned around the area to see if there were any eyes staring back at her and as a figure moved from behind a tree, she screamed.

"Sylvia, stop! It's just me."

Luke came over and crouched down beside her but she was still trembling with fear. "I'm sorry, I thought you would've heard me coming. I had to be careful in case anyone saw me, so I was trying to be quiet."

Tears threatened to fall, so she blinked hard to keep them back. She'd been on edge ever since Grace had left her out here and when she'd heard the noise, fear had completely taken over.

"I'm fine." Her voice shook as she tried to

smile and assure him she was all right. But she was almost certain even he could hear her heartbeat that was pounding in her ears.

He moved over and sat beside her on the overturned tree. "I guess I should have called out to let you know I was coming. I walked my horse in, so it must not have been as loud."

"It's all right. I'm just a bit jumpy, I guess. I've never spent the night by myself out in the wild like this."

He watched her carefully, then nodded. "No, I suppose not. Another thing I maybe didn't think through clearly." He looked back at the fire, picking a small broken branch up off the ground and snapping it in half as he sat lost in thought.

She took the time to stare at his profile, noting the strong line of his jaw that she'd never really noticed before. His hat was pulled down, almost covering his eyes but she could imagine them in her mind. By the amount of dark stubble lining his cheeks, she knew he hadn't taken the time to shave today.

"You know, it's not too late to just take me back. I'd be the one to face the charges for escaping and I promise I'd never say anything about you or Grace helping me. I couldn't live with myself if either of you got into trouble because of me."

He lifted his gaze and looked at her, taking her breath away when his eyes found hers. In the flickering firelight, she was unable to move or look away.

"I'm not taking you back there. I've spoken to Judge Hargreaves and he's going to spend a few days here while I search for you. I've told him what I believe and I know he'll take my words into consideration. He's a fair man and, once I have the evidence to prove your innocence, I'm sure he'll drop any charges of you escaping. He'll understand why you had to do it."

Swallowing, she hugged the blanket tighter and looked down at the fire. The flames were hypnotizing, slowly moving and swirling as she struggled with her thoughts.

"And if you can't find the proof? Will you just let me go?" she spoke the words quietly, afraid of what she would hear. Even if he did, where would she go? And if he didn't, she knew she'd likely be hung and that thought terrified her.

He didn't say anything for a while and suddenly his arm came out and wrapped around her shoulders, pulling her into him. She let herself slump into his embrace, taking the comfort he was offering her. His fingers came down and lifted her chin to make her look at him.

"I promised I was going to help you and that's not something I will ever go back on. I'll find the proof but, if I can't, I'm not just going to leave you to spend the rest of your days hiding."

"But..."

He shook his head and before she could say another word, his lips were on hers. Her hands reached out and grabbed the opening on his vest, desperately trying to hold on so he wouldn't go away. His hand went around her back, pulling her closer, while his fingers traced a trail up her spine and into her hair.

As quickly as it happened, he pulled back, staring down into her upturned face. "I'm sorry. I shouldn't have done that."

Her lips were still parted as she struggled to stop the world from spinning around her. Pushing herself back, she reached up and patted at her hair, trying to get her breathing under control. Her cheeks burned with embarrassment. What kind of woman sat kissing the sheriff who was in charge of arresting her for murder?

"You must think I'm no better than my mother. I assure you, I don't sit around kissing men all the time."

He was still holding her, and he smiled as he shook his head slowly. "No, I don't think you're like that at all. I think you're a woman who has been through a great deal and I should have respected that."

Finally letting her go, he went back to staring at the fire. She didn't know what to say. In all her life she'd never had a man treat her with respect. Her heart was bursting with something she couldn't understand as she watched the reflection of his face in the firelight.

"You can crawl in and get some sleep. I'll stay here until the sun comes up, so you won't have to be out here alone in the dark."

He hadn't lifted his eyes from watching the fire as he spoke and she had to fight the urge to reach out and let him kiss her again. But she knew he was struggling with whatever he was feeling while knowing she was still a woman charged with murder.

He was being forced to choose between any feelings he might have for her and following the law he'd sworn to uphold.

"Thank you, Luke."

She was thanking him for everything—for believing her, for giving her this chance, and for knowing how afraid she was to stay out here alone. There weren't the words to thank him enough.

Crawling back into the cave, she wrapped the blanket tightly around herself for warmth and swore to herself that, somehow, when she got out of this mess, she was going to repay him for the kindness he'd shown her.

Lying in the darkness of the cave, with the lamp turned down low, she could hear the crackling of the fire outside. Just knowing Luke was there gave her the comfort she needed to finally sleep. As her eyes closed and her body started to give in to the exhaustion, she smiled when those familiar eyes filled her mind.

She pushed away the thoughts that kept trying to get in, knowing she was falling hopelessly in love with Luke Hamilton. But what could she offer him?

A life on the run from the law, away from the family he'd finally settled down with? Or with the accusing stares of those who would never believe she was innocent?

No, for tonight, she was only going to think about the good things. And that meant imagining the man out there holding her in his arms and never letting her go.

CHAPTER 12

"So, do you want to tell me exactly what we're doing out here? I'm almost certain we aren't really going to be searching for your escaped prisoner."

Colton and Titus had come with him today when he'd told the judge he was going out to look for Sylvia. They'd been riding silently through the trees for about an hour now and he felt bad knowing he wasn't being truthful to them.

For some reason, Luke was getting the impression from Judge Hargreaves that he wasn't really too concerned about finding her. He hoped that boded well for her chances of forgiveness when he did have to bring her back in.

Once he had the proof he needed, she could hopefully be granted a pardon. And then she'd be free to leave if that's what she wanted. Luke ignored the thought, knowing it wasn't something he should even be thinking about right now. All that mattered was clearing her name.

"What makes you think we aren't searching for her? The judge is waiting for her and if we don't find her, both Grace and I could end up in a lot of trouble."

Titus laughed loudly. "I may not be the smartest man on the planet but I can tell when someone is acting. I was there when you found out Sylvia was missing and since I know you aren't the kind of man to just shrug your shoulders and say, 'Oh well,' I'd be willing to wager my farm that you already knew she was gone."

Luke ignored Titus and kept his eyes focused ahead. He'd make sure they didn't go anywhere near where the cave was located. Grace had taken her out some food this morning after he'd returned and was spending the day with Sylvia.

Colton laughed too as he shook his head. "And Grace came into town earlier today than she normally does and unless she's gone missing too, it seems a bit funny that she wasn't hanging around your office like she normally does."

Luke rolled his eyes and just kept riding. They could think whatever they wanted.

"I mean, don't get me wrong. I'd have likely done the same thing but I have to say I'm shocked that you'd do it. You've been pretty serious about upholding the law since you took over sheriff duties in town."

Luke turned to glare at Titus. "I *am* serious about upholding the law. And what I did or didn't do for my prisoner is nobody's business but my own. Besides, it's best if you don't know everything so that if it comes time to speak to the judge yourselves, you won't be forced to lie."

Colton and Titus looked at each other and shrugged. "So, what exactly are we doing then?"

"I'm going to Duncan Coulter's farm to see what I can find. Every time I go, Randolph won't let me go into the house or do any kind of looking around the place. I need you both to keep him occupied while I search for something that could be used as evidence."

"You're breaking into his house?"

Luke sighed loudly and turned in his saddle to look at Colton. "No, I'm looking around in *Duncan's* house. Not Randolph's. He lived with the mother in a small cabin on the property although I understand they've now moved up into the big house. As far as I'm concerned, that house still belongs to the man whose murder I'm trying to investigate."

"You're in love with that woman, aren't you?"

He ignored Colton's voice and dug his heels in harder, sending his horse flying down the road with a cloud of dust behind him. But before he could get too far, Titus and Colton caught up to him, pulling in front and forcing him to stop. He pulled on the reins, making his horse do a little dance as it fought to keep going.

"What are you doing? Are you trying to get me killed?"

Titus got his horse under control and rode over beside him. "No, we aren't trying to get anyone killed but we need to make sure you've thought everything through. You're putting a lot on the line by helping that woman escape and then going snooping around another man's house for evidence. What if she's lying to you? What if she really did murder Duncan and now you're being played for a fool?"

Luke wanted to reach out and punch Titus Caine right in the mouth. Colton shot an annoyed glance at Titus, then turned to face him. "What Titus is trying to say, but perhaps didn't put the words as nice as others might do, is that we want to make sure you know what you're doing. You could face a lot of trouble over a woman you don't really know. We just want you to be careful, that's all."

Titus shrugged. "That's what I said. He's a grown man, so there's no reason to sweeten the words."

"Listen, I appreciate your concern. However, as Titus has mentioned, I'm a grown man. I know what I'm doing. You're right—I don't know Sylvia very well. But what I do know has told me the kind of woman she is. She didn't kill Duncan and if I won't help her, then who will? She has no one else. You know as well as I do that if they take her off to Oregon City, they are going to want to make an example out of her. She won't get a fair trial and we all know it. There are too many men who will want to make sure she pays."

They sat on the edge of the road, listening to the horses stomping the ground and the leather of their saddles creaking beneath them. Finally, Colton nodded. "I've known you a long time and I know the kind of man you are. If you believed there was any chance she might be guilty, I know you'd do everything to uphold the law. So if you're sure she's innocent, then you've got my help."

Titus sat for a bit longer, then nodded too. "I guess we'd better get out to the Coulter farm. You don't need to think I'm letting you both have all the fun without me."

Luke grinned at the two men with him. He was glad to have them as friends and knowing they trusted him made what he was doing a bit easier to live with. He knew he wasn't exactly following the law by coming out to snoop through Duncan's things but Randolph had left him no other choice.

Sometimes, the law was made to be broken.

CHAPTER 13

The cool water kissed her skin and she let her head fall back so all of her hair would be under the surface. She knew she couldn't stay in the creek much longer because it would be dark soon and truthfully, it wouldn't be too long until her skin became numb from the cold.

But right now, it felt like heaven and she didn't want to move. Getting the dust and dirt from her body was something she'd been waiting to do since the moment she'd stepped off that stagecoach days ago.

Since then, all she'd had time for were quick wipe-downs with a wet cloth. Her hair hadn't been washed in what seemed like months now and just getting her entire body covered in the sweet-smelling soap Grace had brought for her was truly the best she'd felt in days.

It was funny how just getting clean again could give her a new sense of hope.

She sunk down into the refreshing wetness, lying back and closing her eyes. Sylvia let herself enjoy the peacefulness of the world right here around her, letting her worries go for a brief moment. The birds still chirping in the trees above her seemed to be singing their song just for her. There was a slight breeze as the evening approached, moving the leaves in the bushes lining the edge of the creek.

Suddenly, the sound of a horse approaching interrupted the quiet, so she sunk down as low as she could, making sure her body was covered by the water. Crossing her arms in front of herself for extra protection, she tried not to move. If it wasn't Luke, she was going to have to hope whoever it was wouldn't see her.

And even if it was Luke, she was now stuck in the middle of this creek completely naked while her towel sat up on the rock at the edge. As she sat perfectly still, hoping whoever it was wouldn't see her, the water seemed to get even colder. Her body started to shiver, and she looked over at the warm towel and wondered if she could try getting to it before she got caught out here.

As soon as she had the thought, the familiar sight of the hat on Luke's head came into view on top of the horse. He hadn't seen her yet and, as he dismounted, he called her name out quietly.

Clenching her eyes tight in embarrassment, she knew she was going to have to answer him.

"I'm over here, Luke. But don't come too close. I'm...I don't have any clothes on."

He'd already started on his way over when she'd started to speak and before she could finish he'd come around the edge of the bush separating her cave from the creek, he stopped dead in his tracks.

His eyes locked on hers, and immediately her cheeks started to burn. "I...um...I didn't think you'd be here until dark. Grace left a little while ago, and she left me some soap, so I thought I'd get myself cleaned up."

Finally, he seemed to come to his senses again and he turned around, putting his back to her. "I'm sorry, I didn't mean to intrude on your privacy. I'm not sure it's safe, though, for you to be out in the middle of an open creek where anyone could have come across you."

"Can we talk about this *after* I get out of this

frigid water? I feel like my skin is about to go numb from the cold."

His laughter reached her ears and he nodded. "Well, you're welcome to get out any time."

"*Well*, I can't really do that with you standing there."

He shrugged. "I'm not looking."

Sighing loudly, she clenched her jaw together in frustration. "Why can't you just go up to the camp and wait? I will only be a minute."

"I really shouldn't leave you down here alone. That wouldn't be very gentlemanly of me."

Why was he acting so strange? Last night, they'd shared a kiss and he'd left as soon as the sun rose. And now he was teasing her and being downright annoying.

Well, she wasn't going to wait around to figure it out. She was certain her blood was about to completely freeze inside her body. Slowly, she started to make her way to the shore, the sound of the water sloshing around her legs as she walked seemed to echo off all the trees around them. She kept her eyes on Luke's back, carefully edging her way closer. When she was almost out of the water, she ran to her towel and quickly wrapped it around her body.

Her hair was dripping but she didn't dare take

the time to dry it. She would do that after she got her clothes back on.

"So, I went out to Duncan's farm today and did a little snooping."

Her head whipped up as she worked the towel quickly over her wet skin. He still had his back to her and was now leaning against a tree like he didn't have a care in the world. Of course, it wasn't him standing here having a conversation without any clothes on.

"I thought Randolph wouldn't let you look around?"

"No, he hasn't been willing to let me get much of a look but luckily for me, today he was preoccupied discussing some potential business dealings with a couple of friends of mine."

Pulling her shirt over her head, she quickly worked the buttons closed. "What did you find?"

"If you'd hurry up and get dressed, I'd tell you."

She brought her skirt up and tucked her blouse in before reaching behind to do up the waist. Now that she was completely dressed, she sat down on a rock to pull on her stockings and boots. "I'm decent now, you can turn back around."

Luke had already seen her at her worst, so she

figured he could handle seeing her ankles and part of her leg while she finished. She wanted to hear what he'd found and didn't want to wait any longer.

When he turned around, he stared at her for a moment before coming over and sitting on a rock beside her. He had a small notebook in his hands.

"What's that?"

He looked at it for a second, then reached over and handed it to her. "It's not proof but it does give enough doubt that I'm sure the judge would at least consider it."

She sat with her bare feet still sticking out from under her skirts and started flipping through the pages. "It's a journal." She looked up at him. "Is this Duncan's?" As soon as she'd seen the writing, she'd known it had to be his. It was the same handwriting as in the letters he'd sent to her.

Luke just nodded, then reached over and started turning the pages, his hand brushing against hers. Swallowing, she slowly looked up and found herself in his eyes again. His hand rested against her own, then finally he moved it and pointed to the page. "Read this page."

Sylvia tore her gaze from his, her heart racing

as she wondered what Duncan would have written.

Today I put out an advertisement for a bride. Randolph and Winnie aren't happy about it. They keep saying I'm only doing it to spite them, so they won't be left with anything if something should happen to me. And truthfully, that is one of the main reasons I'm doing it. Of course, I wouldn't be opposed to finding a woman who I could fall in love with and possibly have a family with some day.

However, I have my worries about whether that will ever happen for me. Ever since Randolph and my step-mother arrived in Bethany, they've made it clear that they've never forgiven the fact that my father left all of his wealth and possessions to me. Winnie hates the fact that Randolph didn't get anything, even though he shouldn't have been entitled to anything. It's not like he was my father's son. He's my step-brother, and nothing more than that.

I've tried to be kind and offer them a home, but as time goes on, I can see the anger festering below the surface. Sometimes, I even worry for my own safety.

Once I'm married, I will know that even if something were to happen to me, my things will never fall into the hands of those two. So when my bride arrives, I will be sure not to even let them know I'm married until it's too late for them to do anything about it.

Maybe then they will realize that they aren't entitled to anything they haven't worked for. And hopefully, they will move back east and let me live my life in peace. If they don't, I just hope they will leave me and my new wife alone.

Her eyes lifted, and she brought her eyebrows together in confusion. "He'd never told me Randolph was his step-brother. I just assumed he was his brother in blood."

"We've all just assumed that but I guess since no one ever asked, the truth had never come out."

"But surely Randolph still wouldn't have been able to do anything to his step-brother? Just because he wasn't blood, he was still family. You don't think he did it, do you?"

Luke nodded. "I do."

CHAPTER 14

He had to get his thoughts together and stop letting them wander back to the edge of that creek bed when he'd come around the trees and seen Sylvia in the water with her hair hanging in wet curls around her face. Her cheeks had been red from the coldness of the water but her eyes were bright as they'd shone back at him.

He'd always thought she was a beautiful woman but seeing her up to her neck in water while she tried to cover herself had shown him just how stunning she truly was. When her eyes had spat fire at him, while telling him to turn around, he'd witnessed a side of her he hadn't been able to see while she'd been locked up.

As he walked up the street to the boardinghouse, he smiled and waved at neighbors as they called out to him. Guilt ate at him as he thought about the rules he'd broken with these people who had put their trust in him to uphold the law. No matter what the reasons, he knew it didn't excuse what he'd done.

Seeing the judge just coming out the door, he hurried up to him. "Judge Hargreaves, can I have a word with you?"

"Of course, Sheriff Hamilton. I was actually just on my way to your office to see if you'd found any leads on the woman."

He shook his head, his stomach coiling with guilt. "Nothing on her but I have found something I'd like you to take a look at. I've told you my suspicions about Mrs. Coulter's innocence and I believe I've found something that should put some doubt in your mind about her involvement."

Handing the journal over to the judge, he opened to the pages he'd marked. There were a few other entries Duncan had made talking about his suspicions that Randolph wanted what he still felt he'd been entitled to and how he planned to get his hands on some of the land and money Duncan had.

While wagons rolled past them on the street

and people walked by shouting their greetings to the men, Luke was barely breathing as he stood watching the judge. He wasn't sure if he was going to find any more evidence than what the judge was holding, so he just hoped it would be enough to put at least a bit of doubt in the man's mind about Sylvia's guilt.

"Where did you get this?"

Judge Hargreaves lifted his eyes to meet his. There was no sense in lying to the man because the truth would come out eventually.

"I went into Duncan Coulter's home to look around. Randolph wouldn't let me investigate, so I took matters into my own hands. I'm not about to let someone be charged with a crime they didn't commit, any more than I'm willing to let someone go free if they are guilty. In order to make sure I'm doing my job, sometimes I have to do things my own way."

The judge watched him carefully, then nodded. "And I suppose Randolph doesn't know you've got this notebook from the house?"

Luke shook his head. "No, sir, he doesn't."

The other man looked back down at the notebook in his hand. "I don't imagine he's going to be happy about it but we can't ignore what we have here. Do we know if Duncan Coulter had a will?"

"Not that I could find. Unless he was keeping it somewhere else."

"Well, let's see if we can find one."

Luke smiled as he nodded at the man. Judge Hargreaves was prepared to listen to other options, so at least it was a start in clearing Sylvia's name. They started walking back toward his office when he heard his name being shouted.

"Sheriff Hamilton, why are you just walking around town like nothing has happened, instead of going out looking for the escaped prisoner? By now, she is likely all the way back wherever she came from, laughing at how she fooled the small-town sheriff who believed she was innocent."

Luke marched over to Randolph who was standing on the street in front of his office. "I don't need you telling me how to do my job."

"Men, we need to focus on finding out the truth of what happened to Duncan Coulter. I'm sure Sheriff Hamilton knows what he's doing." Judge Hargreaves met his eyes and Luke almost thought the man suspected there was more going on but was letting him know he trusted him to do what he had to do.

"I'm actually glad to see you've come into

town. It saves me from having to send someone out for you. We need to discuss what we've found in this notebook left by your brother. There's some information in it that has me a bit concerned." The judge held up the notebook he was holding.

Randolph pulled his eyebrows together in confusion. "What's that? Where did you get it?"

"I got it from Duncan's house. It was under his bed."

Fury flashed in Randolph's eyes and, for a moment, Luke could see the rage the man possessed and was able to understand how scared Sylvia had to have been when confronted by this man that day.

"What were you doing in my house?"

Randolph spoke the words low and Luke was glad the judge was here to witness the man's anger.

"It is still Duncan's house and since you weren't allowing me to investigate, I decided I owed it to the man who was killed to make sure I did everything I could to bring his killer to justice."

"You had the killer. But you let her go."

Luke was sure if the judge wasn't standing witness to what was taking place, Randolph wouldn't have been able to control his anger. And Luke had a feeling when the rage took over, Randolph would be a hard man to beat.

"That's enough. We aren't going to solve anything like this. I'm taking this notebook inside and I'm going to read through it all. And when I'm finished, I'm going to have some questions for you. But for now, go home and let Sheriff Hamilton do his job without interference from you."

Judge Hargreaves pushed past Randolph to go into the office, leaving the other man glaring at Luke. "You won't get away with it. I know what you've done. That woman will pay, one way or another."

"Are you threatening me, Randolph? Or Sylvia? Because if you are, I might have to let you cool off behind the bars of the cell you were so quick to throw her into."

The man's face was purple and the veins around his temples stuck out as he stood fighting his anger.

"This isn't over."

He turned and stormed away and dread pooled in Luke's stomach. He knew he shouldn't have pushed the man but there was just something about him he didn't like. He was going to have to be careful and watch his back closely.

And, he also knew he was going to have to make sure Sylvia was safe from that man. As long as she was on her own out at that camp, with only Grace to keep her company during the day, she was in danger of being found.

It would be safer for her back here. At least he could keep an eye on her and, hopefully, the judge would be willing to let her stay until they'd found out the truth. From what he'd seen so far, he believed the judge was going to be fair.

He just needed to figure out how to bring her back in without her facing even more trouble for escaping.

Cursing under his breath, he knew he'd made a mess of things. Now he needed to figure out how to fix it.

CHAPTER 15

"I can't go back there. You know what will happen to me if I do."

She turned her back to Luke and went to stand over by the tree that looked onto the creek. The past two days out here had been surprisingly soothing to her, even when she'd been alone.

The thought of going back to stare through the bars of that cell terrified her. She wouldn't be able to feel the breeze on her cheeks or listen to the birds as they kept her company in the trees. She couldn't imagine not being able to hear the water trickling over the rocks in the creek as she fell off to sleep at night.

Luke came up behind her, taking her by the arm and turning her back around. "Sylvia, I promised you I'd take care of this. I've already spoken to the judge about the notebook we found and I'm confident that he isn't going to send you away now until he knows for sure what happened to Duncan. There's enough doubt there now that he knows he'll need to find out more before you can face trial."

She swallowed, staring into his eyes. He'd done so much to help her and she couldn't understand why.

"Why are you helping me so much? I still don't understand why you would do all of this for a complete stranger."

His eyes stayed on hers, the muscles working in his jaw. His hand went down to take hers in his. She held her breath as his thumb started making circles on her skin.

Finally, he shook his head slowly. "I don't know. I can't even understand what is happening but I know I can't stop thinking about you."

She was afraid to move, not wanting to break the moment between them. He dropped her hands and stepped back, turning slightly to look past her. "I just don't want to see you suffer for something you didn't do."

How could she tell him she hadn't been able to stop thinking about him either and that when she closed her eyes at night, all she could see was his face? She'd come out here just a week ago to marry another man and here she was letting herself fall for someone else already.

Even though she'd never had the chance to know or fall in love with Duncan, it still felt wrong to be having feelings like this for another man so soon.

She walked over and sat on the overturned tree by her temporary home. She placed her arms in her lap and leaned forward.

"I'm scared."

She'd grown up in a brothel, seeing things before she was twelve that most people would ever have to witness in a lifetime. She'd fought off advances by men three times her size and had managed to keep herself away from the life her mother pushed so hard to bring her into.

Then, she'd taken matters into her own hands and had traveled west to marry a complete stranger, taking the chance that she would find the love she'd been looking for her whole life.

But right now, she was scared. In all her life, she didn't remember when she'd been so afraid for her future.

Luke came and sat down beside her, resting his elbows on his legs. "I know you're scared but I promise I won't let anything happen."

She turned to look at him. "How can you promise that? I know I have to go back to face the judge for escaping but what if he's so angry about what I've done that he isn't willing to listen to my reasons?"

He was looking straight-ahead, the muscles in his jaw moving as he thought about what to say. "We'll just have to tell him the truth—that I set it up for you to get away."

"No! We're not doing that. I don't want you or Grace getting into trouble because of me. I could have always refused when Grace told me the plan that morning. You could lose your job and both of you could end up in jail too. I'm won't do that."

"You can't stay out here anymore, Sylvia. I don't trust Randolph and I'm afraid if he, or anyone else finds you, it won't be a good outcome. At least at the jail, I can keep an eye on you and keep you safe."

She knew he was right. If Randolph found her out here, he would make sure she suffered. It was too much of a risk now. She'd go back and face the judge and see what her fate was.

"I will go back on one condition."

He looked at her with an eyebrow raised. "You do remember I'm the sheriff, right? If I wanted to drag you back over my shoulder, I could do that regardless of any terms you might have in mind."

She rolled her eyes at his attempt at humor, then waited for him to agree.

"Fine, what's your condition."

"I'll go back if you promise that even if the judge doesn't believe I'm innocent and decides to take me to Oregon City, that you won't do anything else that will put your job at risk. I don't want you to end up paying too."

He brought his eyebrows together and shook his head. "No. I can't promise that."

"Luke, please. You've already taken more risks than you should have for me and I appreciate it. But if it comes down to it, I just can't live with you losing your job, or even ending up in jail, because you haven't followed the law. It would kill me if I knew I'd cost you everything."

He sat perfectly still staring at her.

"And you have to promise you won't admit to having any part in my escape. I will say I ran from Grace when she wasn't looking. If you say anything that will get you in trouble too, I will deny it."

His eyes were pulled together as he held her gaze. His jaw moved as he struggled against the anger she knew he was feeling. But he had to agree. She couldn't live with herself knowing she'd destroyed his life too.

"And what if I don't agree to these conditions?" His voice was low, barely loud enough to be heard.

Lifting her chin slightly, she turned to look out across the creek. "Well then, I guess you're dragging me back over your shoulder."

CHAPTER 16

He kept his eyes wide, scanning the street as he walked with Sylvia right behind him. He held onto the rope that loosely bound her hands. Grace glared at him as he walked toward the office, showing her displeasure at his plan to bring her back in. When she'd shown up today and they'd told her what had been decided, she'd been livid.

"I hope you know what you're doing. The judge is inside," she hissed the words at him as he got closer. There were a few people wandering around the street, stopping to stare at the prisoner being brought back in to face justice.

As luck would have it, Randolph had chosen this morning to bring his mother into town, so now they were able to witness everything. When he spotted what all the excitement was about over by the sheriff's office, he was running as fast as his legs would take him, leaving his poor mother to try and catch up. Luke stood tall, ready for the confrontation. He pushed Sylvia back farther behind him, making sure she was protected.

"It's about time you found this hussy!" He tried to push past him, turning his words on her. "How dare you think you can escape punishment for what you did to my brother. I will never rest until I see you pay, so even if you try to get away again, know that I will spend the rest of my days hunting you down."

Spit flew from the man's mouth as he shouted over Luke's shoulder. Luke pushed against him to keep him from getting to Sylvia.

"Back off, Randolph. I've brought her back and she'll have her chance to speak to the judge. I'd suggest you stay as far away from me as you can get because I'm this close to locking you up too."

"What are you going to lock me up for? Speaking my mind?" The man sneered at him, then turned his eyes back to glare at Sylvia.

"For beating up a defenseless woman, for starters. Then I'm sure I could find a few other things that would help to keep you there."

Randolph stepped back and looked at him. "You've got nothing on me."

"Not yet."

Just as Randolph was about to start spewing his anger again, the judge walked outside and saw them all standing there. He looked around at each of them, then settled his eyes on Luke. "I assume this is the escaped prisoner?"

"Yes, sir."

He figured if the judge didn't ask, he wasn't going to lie about where or how he'd found her.

Nodding his head, the man turned back around to go inside. "Bring her in here so we can listen to what she has to say for herself."

"You better hurry and get her to Oregon City before they let her escape again. I want justice served and I'm tired of waiting."

The judge stopped and faced Randolph. "Sir, I understand your frustration and your anger over what has happened to your brother. However, I'll be the one making the decisions here about whether this woman will be charged. I won't be harassed into doing something because someone wants revenge. Do I make myself clear?"

Luke fought the smirk that threatened. The

look on Randolph's face was almost worth the price of gold.

"Now, let's find out what happened that day with Duncan Coulter."

❧

HER ENTIRE BODY shook as she recounted everything she could remember from the day she'd found Duncan outside. Randolph had tried to interrupt many times but the judge wouldn't allow it. His mother, Winnie, sat perfectly still with her hands tucked neatly on her lap, not showing any emotion at all.

"I swear, I didn't kill Duncan. I came here to marry him and start a new life."

The judge watched her closely. "And what life were you coming from that would force you to marry a complete stranger?"

She swallowed hard, her heart jumping into her throat. She'd known this would come up but it still wasn't something she wanted to talk about. Her eyes darted to Luke who stood behind the chair the judge was sitting in. He smiled and nodded, telling her to just give them the truth.

"My mom worked in a brothel in Missouri. I grew up there."

Both Randolph and Winnie gasped loudly but the judge just sat and listened, waiting for her to continue.

"I knew it. I knew you were nothing more than a whore after my brother's money."

Before anyone knew what was happening, Luke had Randolph against the wall with his arm pushed on his throat. "Don't you ever speak like that to a woman around me again. I swear, if you do, you won't know what hit you."

He was speaking through clenched teeth, with his face right up close to Randolph's.

The judge stood up and went over beside the men. "If you two don't stop this right now, I'm locking the both of you up, so I can speak to this young lady in peace. Randolph, if I ever hear you calling this woman, or any woman for that matter, by that name again, you'll spend the night in jail. And Luke, I know it can be difficult dealing with pompous heathens like this but you need to keep a cool head, so we can find out the truth."

A smile erupted on her face as she heard what the man called Randolph, so she quickly brought her hand up to cover it before anyone noticed.

"All right, Mrs. Coulter, you may continue." The judge came and sat down across from her, giving her a nod of his head.

"I did grow up in a brothel but I never became what my mother had wanted me to be." Her cheeks burned with embarrassment as she tried to explain it all delicately. "I had to get away, so when I saw Duncan's advertisement, I came out here to be his wife."

She looked over at Winnie, wanting to make the stepmother understand she wasn't the person they believed her to be. She didn't know why it mattered to her so much but she wanted the woman to believe her. "I wasn't after anything more than a man who could be my husband and who I could possibly have a family of my own with some day."

Her voice choked on the last few words as she remembered the hope she'd been feeling as she'd made her way west to get married. She had so much excitement for her future and knowing she could have her own real family and within hours of arriving that had all been taken from her.

She looked down at her hands while she regained her composure.

"I would never kill someone. I could never live with myself if I did something that horrible."

When she looked back up, she shrugged. "I know it looked like I did, but I swear, I had just found him like that."

The judge sat silent for a moment, then turned to Randolph. "All right, Randolph, now it's your turn to give your side. I should let you know, I'm a good judge of character and I can tell when someone is telling me the truth or not. So, think carefully about your answers."

"I don't need to think about what I'm saying, because I'm telling you the truth. I found this trollop..." He stopped speaking when Luke growled at him from the corner. "I found this *woman* leaning over Duncan holding that rock over there, covered in his blood."

He pointed to the rock that Luke had put away for safekeeping, which was now sitting on the desk between them. "I don't know how she managed to do it but she killed him. I'm as sure of it as I'm sure the sun sets in the west."

Listening to Randolph, Sylvia had a sinking sensation in her stomach. Either he was really good at lying or he really didn't kill Duncan. So if he didn't do it, and even she found herself believing him, then what chance would she have to prove to the judge that she didn't do it?

She looked over at Luke and her chest clenched. By the look on his face, he was thinking the same thing as her.

"Well, it looks like we've got two people

telling pretty much the same story. Except they both came across the body of Duncan Coulter at different times. So that leaves me to wonder if it was just an accident. Or, did someone else kill him?"

Everyone looked at the judge, unsure what to say now. There wasn't any evidence for anything—it was all just one person's word against another.

"Mrs. Coulter, would you like to add anything?"

Sylvia shook her head, unsure what the judge wanted to hear. "I don't really know what else I could say, Judge Hargreaves."

He smiled at her and shook his head before turning his head to look at the other woman in the room. "No, I mean Winnie Coulter, Duncan's step-mother."

CHAPTER 17

What was the judge getting at? What would Winnie Coulter possibly know? Luke wasn't even sure the woman's mind was all there. Any time he'd seen her, she barely spoke and seemed lost in her own world. That day at the jail had been the only time he'd seen any emotion from her.

His eyebrows came together as he looked over at her. *Did* she know something?

The judge leaned back in his chair and waited for the woman to speak. When it was apparent she was choosing to stay quiet, he asked her again, "Mrs. Coulter, you were there that day too. Can you tell me what you saw?"

She continued staring straight-ahead and he almost started to wonder if the woman was deaf.

Finally, she turned her head and he still saw no emotion in her eyes at all.

Walking toward her, Luke leaned against his desk. "Mrs. Coulter, you do understand that Randolph could be in a lot of trouble, right? According to the notebook we found, Duncan was afraid for his life and felt that you both were after his money."

Winnie Coulter met his eyes and he was taken aback at the coldness he saw. "It wasn't just his money. That money was just as much mine and my dear son, Randolph's. Just because we weren't blood, doesn't mean we didn't have just as much right to everything. But my *loving* husband, Leonard, decided to punish us and leave us with nothing."

"Ma? You don't need to tell them anything about our circumstances." Randolph was looking at his mother in confusion.

She faced him and smiled and it was the first time Luke noticed any kind of emotion on her face. "Randolph, I just wanted you to have what you were entitled to. Leonard had no right to keep it from you."

"What are you saying, Mrs. Coulter?" Sylvia had leaned forward, carefully listening to the woman speak.

The older woman just laughed as she looked at Sylvia. "Do you think I was going to let you get your hands on everything? You gave me the perfect way to fix the horrible situation we'd been put in."

Everyone in the room was in shock, no one saying a word. Finally, Luke spoke, breaking the silence, "Mrs. Coulter, what did you do?"

By now it was quite clear the woman was unstable, so they had to be careful not to set her off. If they did, she might not tell them anything.

But he soon realized she was so far gone, she was already back to that day. "I went out to talk to Duncan, to reason with him. He'd never treated me like a mother and had shown nothing but disdain to me over the years. I told him we didn't want everything, just what was owed to us. He laughed in my face. I was so angry. As I stormed away, I saw a rock lying on the ground. Knowing his chivalry would force him to help me, I pretended to fall and hurt myself. When he came and bent over to pick me up, I brought the rock around hard on the back of his head." She gave a chilling laugh.

"It didn't kill him right off, I had to hit him again while he was stunned. And a couple more times."

Luke's stomach turned as he saw the complete hatred and lack of compassion on the woman's face.

"It worked out perfectly, knowing everyone would assume the new wife did it. Then, my Randolph would get what he was owed."

"Ma...how..." Randolph's voice trailed off as he went and sat down on an empty chair, dropping his head into his hands.

"All Duncan had to do was give us what we should have been given when Leonard died. Your father, Archie Brewer, God rest his soul, never left us a penny. The only reason I married Leonard Coulter was so I knew we would be taken care of. I wanted him to treat you like his own son, but he never could."

Luke turned to look at Sylvia, his heart racing as he realized she was now free. She was still sitting and staring at Winnie, tears running down her cheeks.

"Mrs. Coulter, you took your step-son's life and were prepared to let me rot in prison, or even hang, for the crime you committed. You took away our chance to start our lives together, all because you were so greedy you thought you were entitled to money that wasn't even yours." She stood up and walked toward the doorway. "I need to get outside and get some fresh air. I can't even stand to be in the same room as these people anymore."

Luke wanted to go with her, to make sure she was all right. He knew with everything that had happened to her the past few days, she was exhausted. But he had to stay here and take statements from Winnie and he was going to have to put her in jail. There would be time to comfort Sylvia after he was finished here. He hoped Grace would still be outside, so she wouldn't be alone.

"I did it for you, Randolph. I hope you can forgive me." Winnie still didn't show any emotion and Luke wondered if she even understood what was happening around her. Surely she must not be in her right mind.

"Winnie, you're going to have to come with me. I'm afraid you're going to be spending some time with me here until Judge Hargreaves is ready to take you to Oregon City." The judge went and helped Winnie to her feet, leading her over to where Luke stood holding the cell door open.

The door to his office slammed as Randolph stormed out. Luke would deal with him later. Because even though he wasn't involved in the murder, he was still responsible for the horrible way he'd treated Sylvia when he'd brought her in.

However, even though he still despised the man, he could understand his need to get away from where his mother was being arrested for murder. No one could have faked the shock Randolph had shown when his mother had confessed.

"Well, Sheriff. It looks like your hunch was right. That poor woman wasn't guilty and would've most likely ended up being dragged to Oregon City before we ever had the chance to find out the truth."

"I knew she was telling the truth. Thankfully, everything worked out." He was uncomfortable under the judge's watchful gaze.

"You know, there's still the matter of her escaping."

Luke swallowed hard, his heart pounding as he waited to hear what the judge was going to say.

"But I'd say she's suffered enough. And I'm sure she's learned her lesson. Sometimes, even when you're afraid the judge won't be fair or won't listen to both sides of the story, a person just needs to trust that the man isn't a complete fool. I know the law doesn't always work the way it's supposed to but we need to make sure we always do our best to uphold it." He winked at Luke as he walked back to the desk. "But we also need to follow our gut when it tells us something, even if it might not be the easiest decision."

Did he know that Luke had helped her escape? Was this his subtle way of advising him not to do it again?

He realized he should never have underestimated Judge Hargreaves.

"Now, I'd say there's a little lady out there who could use some comforting. I'm going to start the paperwork here, so I can be on the road to Oregon City tomorrow."

Smiling at the judge, he tipped his hat down in his direction. But before he could get to the door, it was pushed open and Reverend Johnson came in with James O'Hara behind him. "Luke, I think you should see what we found out by the rubble of the church. The last pieces of the mess were being hauled away and there, tucked underneath a board, we found a cloth that smelled an awful lot like kerosene when I picked it up. I thought it seemed odd since it would have been in the area by the backdoor."

Luke took the cloth and held it up to his nose. The pungent smell of kerosene burned his nose.

James came up beside the Reverend and put his hand out toward him.

"What's that?" Luke reached out to take

something shiny from the man's hand. Picking it up, he turned it around to get a better look at it. "A small hip flask." Looking at the Reverend he asked, "Is this yours?"

"No, of course not. I've never seen it before today."

Looking closer, Luke could see something engraved on the side. He wiped the soot and dirt off of it and brought it up to his eyes. The initials R.B. were on the side.

"Who is R.B.?"

Suddenly, it hit him. The man they'd assumed was called Randolph Coulter was actually Randolph Brewer, son of Archie Brewer.

The man they'd just let walk out the door.

CHAPTER 18

"Let go of me, Randolph. My name has been cleared and so has yours."

Fear raced through her veins as the man grabbed her and started to pull her backward. She knew she should have stayed right on the main street instead of walking around back, thinking she could have some privacy from the prying eyes of the townspeople.

"Well, your name might be cleared. But I'm certain it's only a matter of time before your sheriff realizes that in my haste, thinking you'd married, then killed Duncan, I had to get rid of any trace that would prove the marriage happened. I didn't want you to ever see a penny, no matter what any judge might say."

She gasped, staring at him in horror. “You burned down the church, didn’t you?”

Like a kick in the stomach, she realized that because of her, the citizens of Bethany had lost their beloved church.

“I wasn’t taking any chances. And now, even though your name is cleared, you still won’t see any money.”

Getting angry, she pushed herself away from him. “I’ve told you before and I’m going to say it again—*I don’t want Duncan’s money*. I’ve never wanted it.” She laughed cynically. “You never had to do anything. It would have still been yours. But you decided to burn down a *church*. If I were you, I’d say Luke finding out would be the last of my worries.”

He reached out and grabbed her again, throwing her to the ground. As she landed, she slid along the dirt. Pain shot through her shoulder as she hit a rock and a ripping sound reached her ears. She could have cried as she realized this was one of the blouses Grace had given her.

“I told you what I was going to do to you if I ever saw you so much as raise a hand in her direction again.” Luke’s voice roared across the ground to where Randolph stood over her.

She lifted her head, moving slightly to get

away from him. Luke was standing with his gun drawn and pointed directly at the man who was about to kick her. When he realized what was happening, Randolph reached down and yanked her to her feet, pulling on her arm. Crying out as pain shot through her shoulder again, she tried to get her feet under her so he would quit pulling.

He wrapped his arm around her throat and brought her in to his chest, making it difficult for her to catch her breath.

"You've been soft on this woman since the moment you laid eyes on her in the back of my wagon. So what are you going to do now? If you want to get to me, you're going to have to go through her. I don't think you'd want to hurt your sweetheart, now would you?"

His chest rumbled against her back as he spoke and the smell of whiskey mixed with sweat reached her nose. Nausea welled up in her stomach as she struggled to breathe.

"Guess I should've told you. I don't go anywhere without my own protection. And now it's pointed right at her back. So I'd suggest you turn around, *Sheriff*, and I'll just be getting out of your hair."

Her eyes widened as the hard butt of something pushed into her back. She needed to think clearly and try to figure out how to get away from him without getting her, or Luke, shot.

Luke's eyes met hers across the open ground between them, and she suddenly wasn't scared anymore. Somehow, she just knew he would figure something out. She knew there was no way he was going to let this man take her with him and once she realized that, she was able to come up with a plan to help him.

She just hoped Luke would be quick enough to act.

Letting her entire body go limp, she caught Randolph off-guard. He was forced to struggle to hold her up. She knew he'd have to take his eyes off Luke and focus on holding her in front of him.

As soon as she went down, Luke rammed into Randolph's chest, knocking him to the ground. Sylvia twisted out of the way just in time and landed on the ground beside them. The men were struggling and she couldn't tell who was winning.

Suddenly, a flash of black caught her eye between them and a scream rose in her throat as the gun was pointed at Luke. She threw herself at Randolph before he could fire and just as she connected with his arm, he spun toward her.

Pain ripped through the same shoulder she'd hurt when she fell but she knew this was a different kind of pain. It burned and as soon as she looked down, she could see blood everywhere, soaking through the fabric of the blouse.

She fell back, bringing her hand up to try to stop the bleeding while Luke's pained eyes found hers. He was trying to get to her but Randolph was still struggling with him. With one wide swing of his fist, he knocked the other man out cold.

Everything around her was starting to spin, even as Luke was coming toward her. It seemed like he was moving farther away and she tried to fight the blackness that was taking over.

The last thing she remembered was Luke's mouth moving but she couldn't hear a word.

HER EYES WERE heavy even though she was trying to wake up. Her whole body ached and as she tried to raise her arm up to help to get her eyes working properly, she was quickly reminded of what had happened. Whimpering as the searing pain took her breath away, she laid back against the softness of the pillow beneath her head.

"Sylvia? Are you awake?" Luke's voice whispered softly next to her ear. Her eyes were finally able to open and she smiled to see him leaning over her.

"You're okay." She was so relieved to see that Randolph hadn't managed to hurt him.

"I am, thanks to a foolish woman who doesn't have enough sense to let me handle things."

"I had to do something, Luke. He had a gun pointed at you."

Luke rolled his eyes and shook his head as he sat on the edge of the bed. "So, instead you let him shoot you. Do you really think that's something I could live with? Besides, I'm the big, tough sheriff. I'm the one who's supposed to be rescuing the damsels in distress, not having the silly woman risk her life to save mine."

She looked at Luke in surprise. "Luke, you *have* saved me. More times than I can count. Why can't you just accept this one act of repayment from me?"

She grinned at him, trying to ignore the aching in her arm. Looking around, she brought her eyebrows together in confusion. "Where am I?"

"I brought you up to my room. I wasn't about to leave you lying in the street and the cot downstairs was being used by Winnie. Although after the altercation with Randolph, Judge Hargreaves decided it was best to load them both up and get them to Oregon City immediately. He hired a few men from town to help him escort them there."

"So, they're gone already?"

Luke nodded. "They won't be able to bother you anymore."

She looked up at the ceiling, a tear making its way down her cheek as she suddenly realized everything was finally over. But now what?

"Are you all right?" Luke's voice was filled with concern.

She nodded and smiled sadly. "I am but I just realized I have nothing. I have nowhere to go and I don't even know what to do now."

Luke moved closer on the bed and reached down for her hand. "Do you honestly think I'm going to let you go? After everything I've done, everything I risked to get you free, just so I could tell you how much I love you?"

Her breath caught as she met his eyes and she was scared to move or say anything. Did she just hear him right? Her mouth opened to speak but no words would come out.

He just smiled, rubbing her hand with his thumb. "Sylvia, from the moment I saw you lying in the back of that wagon, I knew I was in trouble. There is nothing I wouldn't have done to help you."

"Did you say...you love me?" her voice cracked as she said the words out loud.

He laughed and nodded, tilting his head slightly as he watched her. He wasn't wearing his hat and she had the sudden urge to run her fingers through his thick, wavy hair. But she knew her shoulder would never allow that.

"I did. And from what I've heard, this is usually the time when the other person says it back. That is, if they do." He looked like a young boy waiting to hear if a girl would give him her first kiss.

But this had so much more at stake.

Finally, she nodded, her smile covering her face. "I do love you, Luke. I've never had anyone in my life who has cared about me the way you have. You didn't even know me but you believed me. You took care of me when no one else would have." She grinned up at him. "And besides, I wouldn't just get shot for anyone."

He leaned in closer, gently placing a kiss on her lips. "I'm glad. And now that you're a free woman, I can court you the way you deserve to be. I've already spoken to Grace who is so excited to have you come and stay with her. Both Colton and Phoebe are fine with having you there and said they'll welcome the help with the kids."

She shook her head and laughed. "You've already got everything figured out, don't you?"

Nodding seriously, he kissed her again, this time taking his time as he moved his lips over hers. His fingers came up and caressed the skin on her cheek and he pulled his head back. "I told you, I always have a plan. All I need is for you to trust me."

Her eyes held his and she brought her own hand up to touch his cheek. "I do trust you, Luke. You're the one person I've always known wouldn't let me down."

He swallowed and rubbed his thumb along her jaw. "And I promise I never will."

She stared into the eyes that had reached into her heart and held her prisoner from the moment she saw him. She loved him with her whole heart and she was more than happy to let him have it.

Somehow, she knew the home and family she'd been searching for was right here, holding her now in his arms.

And this was one time she would never want to escape.

EPILOGUE

She stood in front of the brand-new church, painted with the red paint mixture the farmers in the area were putting on their barns. Everyone had wanted this new church to stand out and to be something they could be proud of in their community. They wanted one that people in other towns would talk about and take notice of.

The steps leading up to the church had white railings on either side and, as she waited, she looked around and smiled. Happiness like she'd never known filled her and she lifted her head to the heavens to send up a little prayer.

"I know we never got the chance to know each other but thank you for giving me the chance to get away and

come to Bethany. I hope you can forgive me for falling in love with a man here so soon after your death. This man saved me and showed me how to love. You gave me the gift of freedom from my life back home, and now he's giving me the freedom to live and love. And your name will live on forever here, now that the new church is built. I hope you are all right with how I chose to spend the money you left me. In the short time I knew you, I believe it is what you'd have wanted."

After the dust had settled, Judge Hargreaves came back to town to finish the paperwork and make sure any assets Duncan had were given to Sylvia. The land was sold off and all of the money she received, she'd turned around and donated back to her new community of Bethany to build the church.

This church would have a plaque inside in honor of Duncan Coulter, ensuring his name would never be forgotten. And since the town was continuing to grow, the building was made to also house a new school during the day. Grace had been asked to teach and she was thrilled to have a job where she could be in town to bother her brother every day.

She smiled over at the women standing beside her who were about to become her sisters. Grace had been a friend from the first day she'd arrived in town and Phoebe had quickly become one too. After living out at their farm for a few weeks now, Sylvia had met the entire Wallace family. They'd welcomed her into their lives and she already couldn't imagine her life without them.

James O'Hara came over and put his arm out for her. "Are you ready, young lady?"

Nodding, she placed her hand on his arm and let him lead her up the stairs and into the church. Her breath caught in her throat when she saw Luke standing at the front, his eyes finding hers without hesitation.

Every step she took toward him seemed to take forever until, finally, James took her hand and placed it into Luke's. He smiled down at her, reaching up to tuck a piece of stray hair behind her ear, lingering on her skin before bringing it back down.

Reverend Johnson started to speak and they repeated the vows that would tie them together forever. When the time came to kiss the bride, Luke grinned down at her, quietly whispering, "Well, Mrs. Hamilton, it would appear you're my prisoner once again."

She reached up and threw her arms around his

neck, pulling him toward her. "Well, this is one time I don't mind being held prisoner. There's no one else I'd ever want to hold me."

His lips met hers and she knew, in that moment, her heart would be his forever.

A LOOK AT BOOK SIX

GRACE'S GIFT

CHAPTER 1

"I'm real sorry for putting the frog in Susan's bonnet, Miss Hamilton. I promise I won't never do something like that again."

Grace smiled at the young boy in front of her, standing with his head down and eyes locked on the floor in front of him. "You won't '*ever*' do something like that again, Oliver."

He looked up with wide eyes and nodded his head fiercely. "That's what I said, ma'am. I won't never do it." His eyes darted to the open doorway and the sound of the other children playing outside before they made their way home from school.

She decided not to make this the time to try teaching the proper use of *ever* or *never* in his sentence and let him go join his friends. Oliver was usually well-behaved, and she knew he was a nervous child, so she didn't want to make him suffer any longer. He'd had a rough year after both of his parents died, leaving him to live with his grandmother.

Grace had already spoken to him privately after lunch when the incident happened and he knew he'd done wrong.

"You go on home now, Oliver. And just be sure you remember what I told you. It isn't nice to do something that will scare someone else."

"I know, ma'am. I'm real sorry."

He pulled his hat onto his head and raced to the door, obviously not wanting to take any chances that she was going to change her mind and keep him after school.

She went and stood in the doorway, wrapping her arms around herself and enjoying the heat from the fall sun on her cheeks. The days were still warm, but she knew winter was coming soon, so these were the kind of days to cherish before the cold hit.

Her eyes scanned the town around her and her heart swelled with love. When she'd arrived in this little community of Bethany as a young girl, she never could have imagined how much it would become her home.

She waved at Susan O'Hara who was outside the mercantile she ran with her husband, James. They had become like family to Grace as had so many others in the area.

Of course, her sister Phoebe had married into the Wallace family, who she was sure made up half the population anyway. So, in a way, they were all family.

Wagons bounced past, kicking dust up behind them as they made their way out of town. Some of the children were lucky enough to get a ride back to their farms but she knew many would be walking all the way home. At least she didn't have to worry about them out there on their own when the weather was nice like she did in the colder months.

Grace had been teaching now for almost a full year at this little church which had been built after the community lost the original one to a fire. When the townspeople had rebuilt, they'd made sure it would be able to house a small schoolhouse during the week for the growing population of children in the area.

She still couldn't believe how fortunate she'd

been to be chosen as the first teacher for these children and it was a job she enjoyed more than anything.

She'd never had the chance to attend a proper school growing up, so she was determined to make sure her students got the best opportunity possible. Thankfully, she'd had her mother teach her from a young age until she passed away when Grace was just a child. Then, her sister had taken on the role of making sure she had an education the best she could. When they'd arrived in Oregon, Phoebe's new mother-in-law, Anna Wallace, had stepped into the job of teacher so Grace wasn't left behind in her studies.

Grace was almost certain with so many people involved in teaching her, she'd likely had more of an education than many children at some of the best schools in the country.

She took a few moments to tidy up the classroom to be ready for the morning, then grabbed her shawl from the hook to start making her way home.

Smiling to herself, she thought about the little house she was heading to. It wasn't much and, in truth, didn't have much more than the basic necessities, but the community had provided it for her to save her from having to come all the way from the farm outside of town where she'd been living.

This was her own place.

She'd lived with Phoebe and her husband Colton for the first few years after they'd arrived in Bethany and she was thankful they'd provided her with a home.

But, now they had twin children and Phoebe was expecting another baby soon. Grace knew they needed more space, so when the school board members had approached her, offering her the chance to live in the little house just on the other side of town, she'd gladly accepted.

It saved her from having to ride into town or spend the night at her brother's if the weather was bad. He was the sheriff in town and was now married and expecting a child of his own too.

It seemed like everyone had found someone to spend their lives with and Grace didn't want to be any more of a burden to them while they started their families. She wanted her independence and this house gave her some.

She ignored the little tug in her chest as she thought about how many people she'd witnessed falling in love over the past few years. She hoped someday she might have her own chance but she wasn't sure if it would happen.

There weren't many single men in the area and the one who'd held her heart since she was a thirteen-year-old girl had left town years ago. Everyone still teased her about her crush on Connor Wallace, Colton's youngest brother.

He'd been a few years older than her when they'd first arrived in Oregon, and she blushed as she remembered how relentlessly she'd followed him around. She knew it had likely embarrassed him and she wished she hadn't been quite so fervent in her pursuit.

The thing was though, in her mind at least, it had never been a little crush. Even now, her heart skipped a beat when she thought of him although the memory had started to fade over the years.

She'd been sure what she felt in her heart had been real, even to her young mind.

"Grace! I'm glad we bumped into you. Would you like to come have supper with us tonight at Larsen's Boardinghouse? I've told your brother that, in my condition, I'm too tired to cook a meal today."

Grace laughed as she reached out to hug her sister-in-law, Sylvia, while her brother, Luke, stood beside his wife and rolled his eyes dramatically.

"She's still got a few days to go before this baby comes so I have a feeling we're going to be eating a lot of meals out."

"Well, I've told you many times you both are always welcome to come to my place. I know you haven't been feeling good, Sylvia, so any time you need a break from cooking, just let me know."

Grace knew how ill the other woman had been with her pregnancy and while her brother tried to act like he was annoyed at having to eat out, she knew he'd been doing everything possible to make life easier for his wife. If they weren't going to the boardinghouse or the saloon for a meal, Grace knew Luke had been doing the cooking and everything else he could help with.

"I will, Grace. But I don't like bothering you. After spending all day teaching, the last thing you need to be doing is caring for a pregnant woman who can't seem to stand the sight of most food without feeling queasy."

Grace laughed as Sylvia made a face, trying to make light of how sick she'd been over the past few weeks. "I wonder if it's just my brother's cooking that has caused this particular ailment?"

Luke raised an eyebrow in her direction. "I'm beginning to regret inviting you to join us." Sylvia playfully reached over and slapped his chest.

"Don't listen to him, Grace. I would love your company."

Tilting her head slightly, Grace pretended to contemplate her decision. "As much as I'd love to annoy my brother and join you both, the truth is, I'm quite tired and was thinking of just heading home to have a bowl of soup."

"Well, make sure you stay inside once you get home. You never know who might be coming into town after dark."

Grace rolled her eyes and sighed loud enough for her brother to hear her clearly. "Luke, you know as well as I do that Bethany is perfectly safe. Even when some of the men head to the saloon in the evening, most of the time, everyone is well behaved. It's not like we're living back in St. Louis. Besides, I'm too tired to be out wandering around anyway."

Every night, her brother warned her to stay inside even though there had never been any real trouble in Bethany other than a few fights between men who'd had too much to drink at the saloon. But since the day she'd moved into the little house in town, he'd never stopped worrying.

"I know it's usually safe but you never know who will be riding into town. We've been getting a lot more drifters and strangers stopping around here and the last thing I need is to be worrying about you out on your own."

As if to emphasize his point, the sound of a horse whinnying loudly from the road leading into town interrupted their conversation. Luke squinted to see who it was, then slowly started to shake his head.

Grace turned to see who it was who had her brother so focused. The sun was behind the rider and she struggled to see clearly. She was sure it would be someone from Bethany and not some dangerous stranger who would make her brother's point for him.

"Just as I said. You never know who will be riding into town." Luke laughed loudly and walked toward the rider who was making their way over to them.

"Who is it?" Sylvia lifted her hand to shield the sun from her eyes as they watched Luke step off the wooden sidewalk onto the street.

Grace continued to squint until the rider got close enough for her to make out who it was. Her heart lurched as soon as she saw the man who was grinning down at her brother.

She couldn't believe what she was seeing and

her voice was barely more than a whisper as she replied to Sylvia.

"Connor Wallace."

The man she'd thought about every single day since he left.

AVAILABLE JUNE 2022

ABOUT THE AUTHOR

USA Today Bestselling Author, Kay P. Dawson writes sweet western romance – the kind that leaves out all of the juicy details and immerses you in a true, heartfelt love story. Growing up pretending she was Laura Ingalls, she's always had a love for the old west and pioneer times. She believes in true love, and finding your happy ever after.

Happily married mom of two girls, Kay has always taught her children to follow their dreams. And, after a breast cancer diagnosis at the age of 39, she realized it was time to take her own advice. She had always wanted to write a book, and she decided that the someday she was waiting for was now.

She writes western historical, contemporary and time travel romance that all transport the reader to a time or place where true love always finds a way.

www.ingramcontent.com/pod-product-compliance
Lightning Source LLC
Chambersburg PA
CBHW011451170626
46816CB00009B/2622
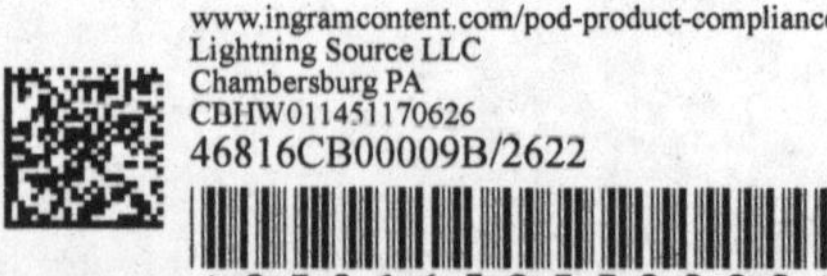
9781639772292